ELEMENTAL
SHADOWS

THE ELDRITCH FILES
BOOK TWO

CALDWELLPRESS.COM

Published by Caldwell Press
Cover Design © 2014 by Lou Harper

Thank you for purchasing and reading Elemental Shadows. It would be greatly appreciated if you could take a moment and leave an honest review of this episode within the guidelines of your favorite retailer.

QUALITY CONTROL: If you find typos or formatting problems, please contact ph8dra@comcast.net so they may be corrected.

If you want to be notified when Phaedra's next novel is released and get free stories and occasional other goodies, please sign up for her mailing list at her website, phaedraweldon dot com.

Your email address will never be shared and you can unsubscribe at any time.

As always, for my father. And the readers.

My grief lies all within, and these external manners of lament are merely shadows to the unseen grief that swells with silence in the tortured soul.

William Shakespeare

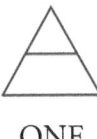

ONE

"You can't possibly understand what I'm going through."

"Sweet Lord and Lady, Robin. You think I've never lost anyone before? What about Ina? What about my mom?"

"It's not the same. You didn't *kill* them." Robin turned as he braced himself against the break room sink. He hung his head. "You've never killed anybody. Not like I killed Kathy."

To anyone coming into this conversation, this wasn't a murder confession. Robin Tremere didn't murder a person—he killed a Changeling, a creature made of Arcane Faerie Magic. That Changeling had taken the place of his niece Kathy, killed her mother, Robin's sister, and nearly killed him. He would have died if I hadn't made a deal with a Leviathan named Dionysus.

But Robin didn't know any of those details. I didn't believe he was ready to know. I'd kept it all hidden within the Witch's world of magic and secrets, in the shadows of reality that permeated New Orleans. It's not that I meant to sound cryptic; it's just that sometimes secrets are necessary.

Like *my* secret. The one where I did kill someone. An innocent. And I used forbidden magic to do it.

And who am I? Samantha Hawthorne, Elemental Witch and said wielder of bad joojoo. Robin and I were in my magic and herb shop, *Bell, Book and Candle*, a little place on Bourbon Street where I lived and worked, saved the world from evil, and sometimes made a small profit to buy food. A few weeks had passed since the incident with the Changelings and Dionysus. The twelve original children the little monsters were created from were still missing, despite my efforts to find them, along with any in the magical community with the ability to Track.

I didn't think telling Robin that Kathy might still be alive was a good idea. I didn't want to give him false hope because I feared Kathy and the other missing children were in *Alfheim*, the Faerie Realm, and if they ate or drank anything, or were favored by the Obsidian Queen, they were probably already transformed into whatever she considered appropriate.

This was just my own worse case scenario. I should have already contacted one of the two Queens, either the Obsidian, Brendi, or the Silver, Tzariene. Winter and Summer. But I had made a deal with the Winter Queen, Brendi, and then reneged on it. The only thing that kept her from taking me and turning me into a horse or a toad or something much worse (I'd been transformed into a stone fountain before so I knew there was a *much worse*) was the Queen's father who had asked Brendi to forgive me.

She did, but I always feared my deal wasn't as much forgotten as placed in a weird sort of forbearance. I mean…she'd tried to make a deal with Dionysus to trade me for a soul. The only that thing that stopped Brendi then was a technicality, which I was damn sure did nothing to soften our relationship.

Robin was the one I was worried about now. Having lost his sister so fast, knowing it was his hand that killed his "niece," and now suddenly taking on the role of uncle—it was too much on his shoulders. He looked thinner, paler, and I noticed the dark circles under his eyes deepening with every day.

He'd come to ask if I could make him a tea or a spell or something that would stop him from feeling.

And that was something I just wouldn't do.

I stood from my chair at the break room table, a large oak handmade work of art, and took my empty mug with me. Robin still had his head bent and he was white-knuckling the marble edge of the sink. I put a hand on his back and rubbed it. "Robin, I'll agree I don't understand what you're feeling. But what I can speak to is the necessity of working through raw emotions. If we never feel or endure hardships, then we never learn from them."

"That's so easy for you to say," his voice was low but his blond hair obscured his face. "You who have all this power, all these things you can do." Robin put his hands to his sides and straightened. The face he turned to me wasn't a nice one. In fact, it wasn't a face I'd ever seen him wear. "Make me forget."

"No."

"But you can do it."

"No. I can't." It was a lie. But it was one of those good lies. It just felt...wrong.

"Then I'm just wasting my time with you." His voice sliced into my heart as he stalked out of the break room, through the door to the shop.

I followed him, calling after him like some lovesick girl. Which in truth I was. "Robin, wait...please!"

Two customers turned to watch us, probably thrilled to have some kind of drama interrupt their morning. I could feel Kyle's eyes on me. He was at the tarot table, helping one of those customers. Kyle Kendrick was my oldest friend and my partner in the store.

"Don't talk to me!" Robin shouted as he yanked open the front door. He turned to look at me. I came to an abrupt stop in front of him, my eyes wide and not liking this side of him. Or this pitiful side of me. "You can help me, but you *won't*. You think my suffering is some kind of noble thing, don't you? Well you can take your magic shit and—"

He didn't finish his sentence and for a half second, I was glad.

But then that half second stretched into a full minute and I realized Robin wasn't moving. His mouth was open in mid-insult, and he wasn't blinking.

"What the hell?"

I turned at the sound of Kyle's voice and noticed the other two customers weren't moving either. Kyle waved his hand in front of the face of the one he was helping.

Nothing.

"This doesn't bode well."

I moved away from Robin toward the counter where I kept my weapons during the day. I couldn't shake the feeling something was crawling up my back, under my shirt. Kyle was right—having Cowens (non-witches) freeze like this inside my own store, within my own wards, was not going to bode well at all. Something was coming.

With a slight surge of my own power I summoned a Fire Elemental, a Salamander, my favorite of the Elemental creatures. My hands should have glowed with transparent red fire.

But they didn't.

Not a single Salamander appeared.

I tried again with a Gnome for Earth, then an Undine for Water. Still nothing.

So I summoned the Element of Air, and to my surprise a small, white swirling image appeared in front of me as Kyle moved in close. I could clearly see the Sylph's face as he stretched his arms and yawned.

"Haven't been using that Element a lot, huh?" Kyle said, indicating the creature's perceived lethargy.

"Shush." I focused my attention on the Sylph who nodded and pointed to the door. With an abrupt clarity and swiftness, I saw an aerial image of four black-clad individuals moving through Bourbon Street without the slightest odd look from tourists or natives. Cloaks billowed out behind them in slow motion and I asked the Sylph to change positions so I could see them from the front.

My skin grew cold and this time it was me white-knuckling the counter before I reached down and retrieved one of my Smith & Wessons.

"What?" Kyle asked to my left. "What is it? I can sense something's coming but I can't see it."

"Yeah," I said as I pulled away from the Sylph's vision and asked the Elemental to stay and witness. He agreed and moved to settle atop one of the crystal balls on the far left shelf. My hands glowed yellow as I lifted the pistol with the name The Lady engraved on its barrel. "We got company all right. Get in the back and fire up your best defense spell."

"What?" But he was moving back to the door to the break room.

Robin and the two customers abruptly turned toward the front in unison, and filed out of the shop without a backwards glance.

I checked my ammo, cocked my wrist so the cylinder would snap back and held the now yellow fiery gun in my hand. I knew what was coming, and Kyle had been right. "Clerics."

This did not bode well.

TWO

If there were a police force, or law enforcement for Witches, it would be the branch of practitioners called Clerics. These Witches were best at tracking, divination, telekinesis, psychometry—most all of the Dianic Gifts. But they were also each Gifted with an Elemental sponsor, which was much different than the usual Elemental Witch like myself.

Clerics, when initiated, were subjected to a brutal and grueling set of tests to both study the candidate's resolve and strength, as well as their brother's and sister's ability at discerning the truth from someone.

In laymen's terms—the initiate was tortured. Magically. Which I hear is pretty damn painful. Regular Cowen (non-witches) tortures are mostly physical. But Clerics deal with truth and punishment on all three facets of the human experience: the physical, the astral, and the mental.

Meaning they fucked you up times three. Ever heard the phrase three-fold?

They take that shit seriously. If a suspect is guilty in any of these states of being, then a Cleric has the right and the training to cap their magic.

As a Hive, a grouping of four, they can also cap an area's magic. It doesn't necessarily mean they remove the magic; they just gum up the works. Which is what appeared to be happening in my shop, hence my inability to summon my Elementals.

Except Air.

Kyle came back out front. "I can't even spark a flame to start incense. Even the water's not working in the sink."

"Area's been capped. It's Clerics."

"Holy Lord and Lady!" Kyle hissed as he looked at the door and noticed my weapon. "Why in the hell are they here?"

I glanced at the Elemental surrounding the crystal on the shelf. Would they be able to sense him? And how was it I was able to summon him, much less *any* magic with a cap in place?

"I don't know."

But I had a suspicion. I believed they were here because I killed an innocent, and I'd used Arcane Magic to do it, which was strictly forbidden. Somehow they had discovered the truth, either on their own or someone had given them just cause to investigate me.

My first thought was that Dionysus had pointed them in my direction. And why not? I was the one Witch who knew the truth, that the Leviathan had stolen the body of my mom's best friend, Inamorata Devonshire, and I had killed an innocent girl. I'd used an Arcane spell from the Malleus Maleficarum, The Witch's Hammer, to strip the innocent's soul from her body. I thought I was exorcising the Leviathan.

I was so...so damn wrong. Instead of destroying the monster that took my mother from me, I'd made that poor soul vulnerable to Dionysus's needs. I'd made that girl a prisoner to a monster in a human body.

This was the secret I kept. This was my shadow.

I knew they were here for me.

But I wasn't going to go quietly. Not when I had innocent children to find and a boyfriend who needed my help, whether he wanted it or not.

The lights flickered and I heard the Sylph's voice in my head saying to put the gun away because the Clerics would see it as a threat. I hid it behind the counter.

The door opened and the four of them filed into the shop. I felt a pressure against my own personal wards, but they didn't penetrate them. Either they couldn't, or they weren't trying. But they were *testing*.

Their hoods were up, and their robes closed. The robes were

floor length and tailored to each Cleric. Each cloak also had a shoulder drape, much like the old depictions of Sherlock Holmes's cloak.

I stood my ground. They stood theirs.

Finally, Kyle spoke up. "Welcome to *Bell, Book and Candle*. I must say I like your robes," he put his hands together. "May I get you some tea?"

"Is that the nephew?" The tall one on the left asked. There were two on either side like bookends.

The other tall one nodded. "He is a Hedge Witch. A rarity in the House of Vervain."

"No," said a female voice. "The Vervains are known for their agility and prowess in Hedge Magic. This one's rarity is that he is *male*."

I looked at Kyle. He looked…irritated.

"So, no tea then."

They all pushed their hoods back at the same time as if they'd rehearsed it. There were two men and two women. Equal representation of the Elemental Witnesses. Earth and Water were female, while Air and Fire were male. Each Cleric wore a medallion with the corresponding color.

The open door to the break room widened and Grey padded out. Grey was my wolf familiar. My circle of friends were the only ones allowed to call her a wolf because I didn't want anyone alerting the local animal control to a wild animal on the loose.

Grey *could* be dangerous. I'd seen her in action.

But she was mine. And no one was going to bother her. I watched her pad to the edge of the counter and sit between Kyle and the counter wall.

"This is the familiar," the tall one on the right said as he took a step forward. Beneath their robes, each of them wore dark clothing. I couldn't see it well enough to know if it was some kind of uniform. This guy was older than the rest, maybe the Hive Leader. His red medallion indicated a Fire sponsor. He sort of reminded me of a graying Jason Isaacs.

Only not as good looking.

The Air sponsored on the opposite end looked to be in his

mid-thirties. He also looked like he just stepped away from a game of Middle Earth. His hair was so blond it was almost white and pulled back from his head in a long ponytail. His eyes were dark and his brows the same. Great, a Legolas fan.

The two women were just as unique. The Water sponsored with the blue medallion had short dark hair and dark red lips that moved as she smacked on chewing gum. She had to be in her twenties.

The Earth sponsored with the green medallion drew my attention. She looked as old as the Fire Cleric, with long silver hair that brushed her hips as she pulled it from beneath her robe. She also seemed the least mysterious as she clapped her hands together. "Oh Mr. Kendrick, I would *love* some tea. Do you have chai?"

"Yes, I do." Her response to him put a smile on his face.

"Wait," Mr. Fire said with his hand up. "We have business."

"And he's a part of that business. But that doesn't mean we can't be sociable," Miss Earth nodded to Kyle. "You make tea. We'll be right here. Oh and I like it English style."

"We've got unsweetened coconut milk. Is that okay?"

"That's perfect."

I watched the interchange with a worried expression. Once Kyle disappeared behind the door, Mr. Fire was at the counter. Grey was on all fours and growling.

"Tell your mutt to be quiet, or else I'll make sure he stays quiet."

I arched a brow at him. "Grey is a girl, and she can speak for herself. I don't like your tone and I don't like you barging into my establishment, overriding my wards." I knew I shouldn't be speaking to them like this. Every Witch grew up learning about the Clerics. They were the boogeymen of our culture. But if they were just getting rid of Kyle so they could accuse and punish me, I wanted them to get it over with. So provoking them seemed a good way to go.

"We do things our way," Mr. Air said as he moved to stand beside Mr. Fire.

"Oh posh," Miss Earth said as she came forward and offered me her hand. "My name's Emily Pearson."

"Why did you give her your true name?" Mr. Fire's face turned red.

"Because she's not the person of interest, Fred. So take it down a notch. I told you capping this area was just overkill."

"I was making a statement."

I gave him a narrowed look. "What, like I have a small penis so watch my magic?"

Oh, I'd just made an enemy. But learning from Miss Pearson that I wasn't under investigation made me breathe a little easier. I set the gun on the shelf under the counter and raised my hand to shake hers. Her palm was warm and dry. I missed my *dex* not activating and showing me what she was.

"Oh," Emily said and then smiled. "I felt it try. That's a good spell to have auto trigger in your personal ward. Very smart. Just like your mother."

I pulled my hand back. "You knew my mother?"

"Oh yes. Fred and I both did. She was asked to be a Cleric many times, but always refused. So," she straightened her robe. "We should get down to business soon as Mr. Kendrick comes back."

"Why don't we just move this to the break room?" I gestured to the door. "I have a table that will accommodate at least ten."

They all nodded except Fred. He was still eyeballing me. As they filed through the door I looked at the Sylph and invited him to my shoulder. He came with a sprint and settled in my hair. I couldn't exactly feel him, but I knew something was there. I'd done this several times with my Salamander but never with a Sylph. I might have to try it with all my Elementals.

Kyle set out a silver tea service, snacks and everything needed to host a party.

Only this wasn't a party.

Fred insisted on sitting at the end of the table. Since I always sat on the end nearest the door, he sat on the opposite side and scowled. Grey sat at my left and I idly stroked her neck. I could feel her muscles taut and ready under her luxurious fur. She hadn't taken her eyes off of Fred.

After a few awkward moments, and me feeling like the whole scene was too surreal for daytime TV, Emily broke the ice. "Miss Hawthorne...can I call you Samantha?"

"Sam's fine."

"Oh good. Sam, we're here on behalf of the local Eldership to ask you a few questions about Arden Vervain."

Kyle and I glanced at one another. Arden Vervain was the self-appointed Witch Queen of New Orleans, and she was Kyle's aunt. I'd met her twice now.

That was enough.

"What about her?" Kyle asked as he sipped his tea.

"What's Vervain's relationship to you?" Fred asked. He had a lot of tension in that voice.

"She's my aunt."

"Not you," he pointed at me. "Her."

"My name is Sam, Fred. Use it," I continued to pet my wolf. "Arden is Kyle's aunt. There is no relation to me."

"Don't be a dumb bitch—"

"Fred!" Mr. Air said. It was only the second time he'd said anything. And then he looked at me. "We're aware of Miss Vervain's proposition to the Eldership, made during an emergency meeting a few weeks ago."

I pursed my lips. "You mean when the Changelings were attacking their parents and eating people's faces off."

He blanched. Renn Faire boy had a weak stomach. "Yes. During that time Mr. Alfonso Higgins was killed. He was this area's High Witch, in case you weren't aware."

"I was informed of that after he was killed."

"The meeting was held in her home in the Garden District and at that time she promised—"

Fred stood at that moment and slammed his fist down on the table. Grey growled and stood. "Where is that damn head? We know you have it because Vervain said she'd seen it here. We demand you hand it over to the Hive now!"

I was on my feet before I knew it.

So was Kyle.

And the Sylph at my neck was also on alert, whispering in my ear.

I'm usually a pretty patient person. Or I hope I am. I try to be. But this was just out of hand. And getting ridiculously stupid. The man wasn't spouting nonsense though.

Up until two weeks ago I did have a head in my basement. It was the head of the former Obsidian Queen, Medbh. And the head talked. Given the Faerie's inability to lie, if I asked the head a direct question it would have to tell the truth or say nothing.

Most of the time the damn thing kept quiet, but when she did tell the truth, I learned a lot. My biggest complaint about her had been her off-key, colorful rendition of bawdy pop songs.

And she didn't censor.

Did have was the key two-word phrase here. It wasn't there anymore, but apparently that information wasn't shared with the local Magic Benders. "First off, no one gave you permission to invade *my* home and *my* place of business. I am *not* a member of your community, nor do I participate in your archaic foolishness." I said all that as I bent forward and put my left hand on the table and pointed the index finger of my right hand at the table for emphasis.

"Secondly, the head Arden had no business telling anyone about isn't here anymore. It's gone. So you don't have to worry about it anymore."

"Where is it?" Miss Water asked. She and Emily were the only ones still seated. I didn't remember when Mr. Air stood up.

"It's back in *Alfheim*, where it belongs." That wasn't the exact truth. The actual head, which resembled a ceramic doll's, was still in my basement. But whatever part of Medbh had possessed it was indeed in *Alfheim*.

Fred made a rude noise and came from around the table toward me. "You really expect us to believe this nonsense about a fairy place called *Alfheim*? That's bullshit and you know it. You're hiding the head because of its power. And I plan on filing charges against you so I can tear this building apart piece by piece to find—"

He got a little too close as Grey's growl magnified and she leapt from my side at his face.

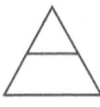

THREE

Grey and the Sylph acted either by coincidence or in unison. Either way, Fred didn't stand a chance.

Grey moved first as she growled, showed teeth and lunged at him. Fred, being a Cleric and Fire sponsored, thought he would attempt to barbecue my wolf.

As I raised my hand to grab at Grey and pull her back, the Sylph assumed I wanted power.

Now, Air can do one of two things to fire. It can feed it, or it can smother it. The Sylph actually used my hand as a conduit to pull the air from in front of the flame so there was nothing for it to feed *on*. Grey wasn't stopped by anything and pushed Fred backward on the floor by momentum.

"Sam! Stop her before she kills him!" Emily said.

I moved to the side of the table to see if Grey was indeed killing him, not that I would have minded. But instead, she had him pinned on his back as she stood on top of his chest like a conquering hero, her snout in his face, growling and drooling on him.

Good girl.

I put my hands on my hips and looked at Emily. "She won't kill him. Grey's not like that."

"She could get put down for attacking a Cleric."

I turned and shot daggers of defiance out of my eyes at Miss Water. "Really? You really want to go there with me?"

"Sam...please...tell her to get off of Fred. He's just a very excitable man."

17

I looked back at Emily. "He threatened me. He threatened to tear down my house and to destroy my life. Why? I told you the truth. I stay out of the community's business, Emily. The head isn't here."

"All right. You say it's back in *Alfheim*."

"Yes."

"With whom?"

"The Obsidian Queen. So if you want it, you have to go through her."

I knew no one in that room was going to mess with Faerie.

I put my hand on Grey's back and she instantly calmed. "Come on girl. You did a good thing. Now come sit with me."

She moved off of him, turned and followed me back to my chair. Once I sat down, she sat down and panted as if nothing had happened.

Emily helped Fred up from the floor. He dusted himself off and glared at me. I glared back at him.

"Okay," Emily started. "Let's move on."

"Not yet," Fred just wasn't going to step away. "How did you manage magic?"

"Excuse me?"

"You used magic to put out my Fire. How?"

I looked at the others. "Anyone see me use magic?" And when I looked at their faces, I realized they hadn't seen the Sylph. In fact, they weren't even seeing him or sensing him now.

How is it an Elemental could hide from a full Hive of Clerics?

The Sylph shifted against the right side of my neck and tickled my ear…and my view of things abruptly shifted.

I could see my hand on the table. Only it wasn't just my hand, but a miasma of sparkling red, like glitter in water. The red pulsed, moved and undulated, not just there but around my thighs, and around the table where I touched it. Even around Grey.

I was covered in it. So was she.

Was that it? They couldn't sense the Sylph because of Arcane? Was I using it now? Had I somehow, subconsciously cast a protective spell that made an Air Elemental immune to the Clerics' cap on magic?

Everyone shook his or her head and the red was gone. It was an instance of time, a millisecond of insight. Had it come from the Sylph?

So I ran with it and gestured at Fred with my hand. "No magic. My familiar was faster than your draw, that's all. And surely you don't mean to be hating on a familiar doing their job of protecting their charge, do you?"

I had him. He sat back.

But he wasn't happy.

He knew something had happened and I knew he wasn't going to let this go.

"Let's move on," Emily said. "I vote to table the discussion on the head. Sam, one of the other things we'd like to discuss is the Malleus Maleficarum."

"The Witch's Hammer?" Kyle blinked at her. He put his hands in his lap. "What about it?"

"It was in Higgins's care but it disappeared not long after Arden Vervain entered Higgins's house."

"You mean the *real* Maleficarum?" Kyle prodded.

Fred snorted. "Oh come off it. We know both of you are aware of the Hammer's truth. And what it contains inside."

Yes we did. But no thanks to any of these Witches. "So we can speak freely about the covens holding an item bathed in Arcane Magic?" I looked at each of them.

The only one that looked apologetic was Emily. She spoke first. "If you know why we had it, then you should understand. It's a powerful book, and something that should be kept safe."

"You mean from the Magicians," Kyle said. He was more talkative than usual. And to Clerics, no less. Weird.

"Well, duh?" Miss Water said from her seat on the other side as she smacked her gum. "Those idiots don't see the dangers anyone faces when using that kind of magic. The price it takes on them."

I had heard about the price of Arcane Magic all my life. And yet I'd used it. I still hadn't seen a price; at least not something physical, or even mental. Maybe it was something spiritual? Like on the astral? I absently toyed with the rectangular silver charm at my neck. It hung there from a black cord.

I'd had a few customers notice it and ask if I was deaf or hearing impaired. Apparently, they saw markings on it that looked like Braille.

To me—I saw it for what it was. It was still a rectangular silver charm, but for me it pulsed red and sparkled with the Arcane Magic it was made with, housed in an ethereal casing of Digital Magic.

Yeah…I was wearing the Malleus Maleficarum around my neck. And no one in the room knew it. Not even Kyle. The only other person privy to this bit of scandal was the Witch who made it.

Ivan Westerfield, my other employee and member of my small group, had called in sick that morning. At the time I didn't think anything of it. But with the Clerics showing up at my door—now I was starting to wonder if there was a correlation.

Not one of these Clerics had noticed the necklace or the Arcane feel and smell of it. Just as a side, Arcane Magic smelled like day-old raw chicken left out in the garbage. And it either looked like sparkling red glitter, like the Wicked Witch of the East's shoes, as it did for me, or it looked like small, writhing red worms. Scarlet dyed maggots was Ivan's best description I think.

I shrugged. "Then why not ask them if they took it?"

Fred sneered. "The Magicians? Please…they're not powerful enough or even organized in a way that would allow them to steal back the Hammer."

"Are you that narcissistic?" I'd really had it with this ass. "You think your shit doesn't stink? Someone took the book out from under your nose. I'm assuming you searched Higgins's house?"

Emily spoke. "Physically and magically. We have come up with nothing. It's our suspicion Miss Vervain took it and is holding it. We want to get it back."

"And no one thought bout the Magicians in the city?"

All four of them shook their heads.

I knew I was playing with dry kindling by throwing out suspicion aimed at our long time nemesis. But really…I'd met some pretty good Magicians through the years. The only difference between them and us was as minuscule as the difference between Baptists and Methodists. Baptists dunk and Methodists sprinkle.

Witches invite the Elementals in to participate in our work, where the Magicians trap them and force them to do their bidding.

It was all kinda B-movie stuff.

"And you're sure Arden Vervain has it?"

"She was in Higgins's house unauthorized after she made her promise. And then again after she failed to deliver the head to the council."

I knew Arden had gone into the house hours after Higgins was reported dead. I wasn't aware Arden went *back* into the house. Kyle and I glanced at each other again. Might be a good idea to find out why Arden had been that careless.

"What do you want from me?" That's what it all came down to, wasn't it? I was feeling a bit cocky myself, since they weren't here to arrest me for using Arcane. Hell, they couldn't even detect it!

Now Fred looked like the Cheshire Cat and I didn't like it. "We're charging you to find out if she possesses it."

"Charging me?" I looked at each of them. "I'm not part of this circus, remember?"

"You're a Witch. And you're an Elemental," Miss Water shrugged. "You don't have a choice. You're a part of the community as much as Mr. Kendrick here."

"No. I'm not." I sat forward, but this time Grey plopped down on the scuffed hardwood floor for a nap. Apparently she wasn't sensing any real danger now. "I wasn't raised in your world. And you weren't a part of mine. So no, my being an Elemental is my business. I do a job. I help people. And I make a living. End of story."

Emily pulled a scroll from her robe and unrolled it. Electronic devices didn't always work with magic, and those who used magic on a regular basis couldn't be near them at all. Normally, I'd be worried about my shop's register and the computer, but I had a secret weapon. Which had just pulled up in the alley behind the building in his truck. I had no way of sending him a message without accessing Spirit.

To my surprise, a tiny white screen with bubbles for text appeared in front of me, like the screen on a smart phone. A new bubble appeared with **I'LL WAIT TILL THE SPOOKS LEAVE**, and then it vanished.

Ivan had sent me a message. *His* way.

"I'm afraid you don't have any recourse in this," Emily said as she read from the scroll. "On October thirtieth of this year, a reported Changeling approached your shop and attempted to enter. This same Changeling was the very one that murdered Higgins in his store before making a straight line from there to you. After that, you went to see Arden Vervain after an Elder Community meeting where you made a deal with her to give her the head—"

"No I didn't—" I said.

"No she didn't—" Kyle said at the same time.

Emily held up her hand. "You will have plenty of time to dispute this record. These are the facts given to us."

"From whom?"

"Arden Vervain. She claims you were helping her track down the book. She also claims you betrayed her and one of your own coven members—"

"I don't have a coven—"

"Please Sam, let me finish. Miss Vervain claims one of your coven members actually stole the book in hopes of framing her."

Kyle and I were on our feet. Kyle went first. "No one here stole that book. We never even went in Higgins's house. That was all my aunt."

"We know," Miss Water said and held up her hands, then lowered them to indicate we needed to sit. When we did, she continued. "We can verify facts. It's what we do. Neither you or Miss Hawthorne were ever in Higgins's house." She leaned her head to her shoulder. "But your other member was."

Shit. Damn. Ivan.

This was the truth. Ivan had been kidnapped and forced into that house because he could actually see Arcane, where others smelled it. He saw it as writhing worms. The scarlet maggots.

I opened my mouth to protest but Emily waved dismissively at me. "We know you filed a complaint with the NOPD. Your shop was vandalized and you reported Mr. Westerfield kidnapped. You blamed Arden Vervain."

"Yeah, she threatened me because she wanted that damn head. And I said no. I never joined up with her or worked with her on *anything*."

"And you still believe Arden kidnapped Mr. Westerfield?"

The answer was no. A Leviathan had taken him. But not one of these guys had mentioned Leviathans, much less Revenants. Both of which were Vampires in laymen's terms. And if you had to color code them, Revenants were technically good Vampires, and Leviathans were…nasty sons of bitches.

I should know.

The woman who raised me after my mother died had been one. In fact, she'd ordered the hit on my mom, Elizabeth Hawthorne.

When did I find out?

Two weeks ago. And I still wasn't over the shock.

"Miss Hawthorne?"

"Ivan said he didn't know who kidnapped him. He was kept bound and blindfolded. He was forced into a house he said he didn't recognize and was told to look for the book."

"Does he have some sort of magic that would make that possible?" Fred asked. He was looking at me funny.

I shook my head. "His Gifts are pretty small. He's Dianic. Just a touch of psychometry."

Emily looked over at Mr. Air and Fred. "That kind of magic could have helped find the book."

"Yeah but I have that Gift and never found it," Mr. Air said.

"Exactly. You'd already looked after Higgins's death and the meeting, and then whoever kidnapped Mr. Westerfield had the same thinking. But it wasn't there," Emily looked back at me. "And he was released back to you?"

"Yes."

"Unharmed?"

"Well no. He'd been beaten. Spent some time on medical leave."

"We'd like to talk to him."

I pursed my lips. "He's not here."

"Yes, he is," Miss Water said. "He's in the back in his car." She frowned. "On his phone. Geez…if he can use a phone like that without draining its battery, then his Gift is weak as hell. Why would anyone wanna use his power?"

Oh man…if only they knew the truth. But I didn't want them to know.

So it was change the subject time. "Why are you so ready to pin this on Arden?"

Fred sneered. I sneered back. "It makes sense you wouldn't have heard, since you consider yourself above us."

I reached over and touched Kyle's arm. He shook his head. "I'm not above anything and I haven't heard anything about my aunt. What are you talking about?"

Emily leaned forward as she rolled the scroll back up. "It's terrible. Simply terrible."

"What?" I said that a bit too loud and maybe with a little too much force.

"Three of the city's Elders have been found dead in their homes since Sunday," Fred crossed his arms over his chest.

Three Elders? Sweet Lord and Lady! Now they had my attention. "You're not saying there are more Changelings killing random Elders are you?"

"No. For each death the cause was ruled as natural causes officially, but unofficially," Fred's harsh exterior cracked. "They were scared to death."

"Huh?"

"What Fred means is, they were asphyxiated. Strangled. There is evidence on all three bodies that someone sat on their chests and strangled them. "

I wasn't a doctor but… "What makes that a natural cause?"

"It was something picked up magically on their astral bodies. Not physically."

Oh.

Emily continued. "And what makes Fred say that is…all three of them had the expression of someone in a moment of fright."

"What…" Kyle said. "Does that look like?"

"I can provide you with pictures if you're into that sort of thing," Mr. Air looked at Kyle.

"Oh shut up, Bilbo," I leaned into the table. "This is serious shit, guys. Three Elders are murdered since Sunday, and you haven't released this to the magical community."

"We're still investigating."

"You're…" I looked at each of them. "You're looking at Arden for this." That…was crazy fucked up. "Arden Vervain? Killing off Elders?"

"Sam," Emily put her hands on the table. "We're just as shocked. But we've conducted forensic magic on each of the victims and on their homes. I'm afraid the last person to see each of them was Miss Vervain. And each of them was in the middle of writing her an email at the time of their death."

An email?

Miss Water stood, and as she came around the table, retrieved a piece of paper from her robe. She handed it to me.

Kyle moved in close and Grey got out of the way. She moved around the other side and sat up to put her paws on the table beside me as if to look at what the paper said.

I opened it.

Dear Miss Vervain,
I am happy to share the news of my withdrawal for consideration of High Witch, and to offer you my support for the upcoming vote.

That was it.

It was a damning piece of evidence.

"You see, Miss Hawthorne," Miss Water said as she took the paper back. "We suspect Arden has the Hammer and is using it to get rid of her competition to seek the position of High Witch of New Orleans."

FOUR

"First up," I said and pushed my index finger against the table. "What makes you think Arden can even use the Hammer? I thought no one could. I mean, it's like a magic sword or a wand, isn't it? Is she pointing it at them and they drop dead?"

Emily shrugged. "I'll admit we're at a loss."

"You're grasping at straws," Kyle rubbed at his forehead. "Have you tested my aunt for traces of Arcane Magic?"

They looked at each other. Kyle and I exchanged a glance and then looked at them. I pointed. "You can't sense Arcane, can you? Not even magically."

"Some of us can smell it. Or they claim they can. But the truth is," Emily looked a bit uncomfortable. "There's no known magic that can detect it."

"Yet," Fred threw in.

I looked at him. "What? You got some Clerics working on such a spell?" Inside I was pretty happy. They couldn't see it! Which meant they didn't know I'd used it. "So...how, as Clerics, have you been preventing people from using it if you can't even tell they have?"

"We didn't say we couldn't tell," Miss Water said. "The stories we teach our children and our community aren't lies or made up, Miss Hawthorne. The use of Arcane does change a Witch."

"Yeah, I was told that too. But I'm starting to get the impression it's not the same kind of change I'm thinking of."

"It's not a physical change. An Arcane wielder's hair doesn't turn colors and their eyes don't start shifting like a Revenant's. It's in their personality. Their being."

Emily leaned into the table and put her hand on the wood. "Sam…Arcane Magic is a shadow on the soul. It takes hold and slowly, over time and use, removes that soul's humanity. This is why we discourage it."

I…didn't know that. And I just got sick in my stomach.

"We're watching Arden Vervain. Keeping an eye on her behavior."

"You're watching my aunt's soul," Kyle's flat tone warned me he was close to being over this meeting.

"Yes, Mr. Kendrick. We are," Emily straightened her back. "There is another matter we need to discuss before we set up your charge, Sam."

Set up my charge? Oh hells bells…they were serious about me finding out if Arden had the Hammer?

"Where is Inamorata Devonshire?"

I'd opened my mouth to keep hammering at Fred, so Mr. Air's abrupt question about Ina came out of left field.

To sum up, Inamorata was gone. She was a Leviathan. And I had no idea where she was. "What has Ina got to do with any of this?"

"Inamorata Devonshire is a Cleric. She'd retired from service but we keep tabs on our own. What pinged our radar was that her group disappeared. All twelve members. Including her. That's twelve missing persons."

I glared at him. It was my go-to reaction when I didn't want to look guilty. Eleven of those members, all Ghouls, had been set on fire by a local detective. The twelfth killed by me. But I wasn't admitting to anything. Not one of those bodies would ever be found.

Ever.

"She's gone?" Kyle said, stepping in for me. "I'll admit we haven't gone to see her since Samhain. Did something happen?"

All eyes locked on him and I took in a deep breath. This meeting needed to end. I had a lot of information I needed to process. And my first order of business was talking to Arden. *Now.*

"Her house is still there. But it's been locked up tight and the security system's on. The magical wards are still in place," Fred looked at me again. Oh goody. "But they have an odd signature."

I shrugged. "So?"

"We know the house is yours. She was your guardian. She's been by your side for eighteen years. But she disappears and you're not even worried," he narrowed his eyes at me. "Why is that?"

"Fred," Emily countered as she turned to face him. "All this is well and good and it might be that Ina and her group took a trip together. But their business is not ours. The question's been raised as promised. Ina's broken no laws and we've seen no evidence of foul play. As far as we know, she might have taken her group on a Yule Solstice trip somewhere. So," she nodded to him in a curt fashion before she turned back to me. "Back to what we were talking about."

I held up my hands. "I do not believe Arden killed three Elders. I mean…why?" I spread out my hands and looked at each of them. "If Arden wants the High Witch position, killing off her competition isn't going to garner her the votes. And if the emails are real—"

"Why wouldn't they be real?" Fred snapped.

I looked at him. "Who's to say whomever broke into their homes and killed them didn't type the letters themselves with the sole purpose of framing Arden Vervain?"

It was apparent on their faces that idea hadn't occurred to them.

"Did the cops dust for finger prints?" Kyle asked.

"I know their forensic team was in all three houses," Mr. Air said.

I put my hand on the table. "Then there you go. Wait for fingerprints," I stood and scooted the chair back. "We're done."

"No, we're not," Fred stood, as did the other Clerics. "You haven't cleared up a thing since we've been here. If nothing else, at least for me, you've raised more questions. Questions I plan on getting answers to."

Emily waved dismissively at him. "Oh pish posh. Not if any of them aren't directly related to why we're here." She looked at me and clasped her hands in front of her. The Sylph brushed against my neck and I nearly jumped. I'd almost forgotten he was there. "We still want you to find out if she has the book."

"But you said she was in Higgins's house and didn't find it."

"She kidnapped your employee, beat him and then took him there."

"There is no evidence it was Arden. I was mistaken." And that was the truth.

Emily shrugged. "He was blindfolded and beaten. He might not know. So we should question him. At another time. For now, Sam, we're going to hold charges until you get back with us on news about the Hammer."

"Charges?" Kyle said. "For what?"

"Harboring a dangerous Arcane artifact," Fred smiled again. "You didn't think you'd walk away from that, did you?"

"I don't have the head. Did you ever see me with the head?"

"No."

"Did anyone ever see the head?"

"No, but Arden swears she saw it."

"The one you suspect of killing off Elders. That's your witness."

I swear I'd just made a seriously bad enemy.

"Guys, it's hard to convict anyone of anything without proof. You've got the word of a suspected murderer. No photographs. No proof. No evidence. You can search my shop if you must, but there is no head here."

"Sam," Emily said. "We have the right to shut you down on just suspicion alone. Now, if you don't help us recover the Hammer, I'm afraid we're going to have to take this to the top and request a warlock."

A warlock? Seriously?

Popular belief it seems was that a warlock was a male Witch. It's not. It's a state of being. And it's not a state any Witch wishes to be in. I'd only met one warlocked Witch and it wasn't pretty. She'd been cut off from her magic, rendered little more than a Cowen. Shunned by her family and friends and left utterly alone in the world.

She barely lasted a week in that state before she took her own life.

"Against Sam?" Kyle moved close to me. "You need a better reason that that. A warlock is something only Parliament can decide and the crime the Witch commits has to pass several rules of judgment. Not finding a missing book is not a reason."

"Noble, isn't he?" Emily pulled her robes around her but she didn't contest Kyle's outburst. Which told me he was right. They didn't have the power to render a warlock on their own or even perform one. All they had was the threat of one to hang over my head. And honestly, I wasn't exactly the most popular Witch in government circles. "The warlock would be for your aunt, Arden Vervain. Not for Samantha, Mr. Kendrick," she looked at me. "You have our request, Samantha. You have twenty four hours to find the Hammer, or at least find out what happened to it."

"Or you'll take my inability to find something I have no control over to Parliament and punish an innocent woman."

Emily smiled. "Good day."

Kyle gave me a helpless look before he escorted them out. Ivan came in through the back door, wearing his usual hoodie, t-shirt, jeans and fingerless gloves. His Japanese American features were twisted up in a serious frown and his thick black hair stuck out at odd angles. "You look like an anime character."

"It's windy outside," he pulled an earbud out. "Did I hear all that right?"

I blinked at him as Grey got up and went to him, sticking her nose in his hand for attention. He instantly bent down beside her and scratched her neck. "You heard everything?"

"Well, yeah?"

"How?"

"The wards. They're like a security system. So I just tap into them like I would an electrical system."

I put both hands on the table. "Is that new? You doing that?"

"Well, yes and no. I tried it when I pulled up because I wanted to see if you and Kyle were inside and it worked. I reverse engineered it. We set the wards. So our essence is in the system. Your essence touched my essence and—"

"There will be no touching of essences," Kyle said as he came back into the break room. "Sam…we can't let them do that to Arden. If they warlock her she'll lose everything."

"I know, I know. Did you lock the door?"

"Yeah, and I hung the lunch sign out," he looked at Ivan. "I thought you were sick."

"I am. Got a massive headache."

Ivan was getting a lot of headaches lately. And I felt guilty about it. He admitted to me a few days ago that the headaches started after he magically digitized the Hammer and stored it in his body. After he did that, I had him upload it and mangle it several times.

This is where I should explain Ivan's Gift. It wasn't what Kyle and I said it was to the Clerics. Ivan wasn't the possessor of a weak Dianic Gift. Not at all.

I was an Elemental Witch, and Kyle a Hedge Witch.

Ivan was a Cyber Witch. He could actually manipulate the web the way Kyle and I manipulated the Elements and herbs. The small rectangular disk around my neck was something he'd made by recoding and manipulating a digital version of the Hammer and then downloading it as an amulet.

Apparently because I'd used Arcane Magic once, I was able to summon the book by holding the amulet in my hand and concentrating on it. I also had to say "open sesame" out loud.

He was working on that part.

Most of this Kyle knew. He just didn't know the Hammer was my necklace.

"Why did you come in?" Kyle held a hand over his face. "I don't want your germs."

"Have you guys been watching the news?" Ivan looked at both of us as he scratched Grey's neck and the top of her head. "What have you been doing?"

"We're not all as interested in current events as you," I moved the chair and then pushed it under the table again. "What's so fantastic that you got off the couch to come in?"

"If I tell you, will you explain what it was I just heard? And what a warlock is?"

Kyle and I looked at one another and nodded. "Sure," I said.

Ivan motioned everyone back into the shop. The lights flickered as the cap the Clerics casted evaporated. He turned on the computer with a touch and then opened a browser. No mouse. He didn't need one. Or a keyboard. I watched as the browser flipped through to a bookmark on the local news channel.

I glanced up at Ivan to see the green sheen in his usual brown eyes.

"What's it look like to you when you do that?" Kyle asked.

Ivan shrugged. "It hard to explain...okay here we go. These are two news reports from yesterday. This first one's in the morning and the other last night."

A video window came up with an article and a byline.

"You guys can read it later if you want, but what it's talking about is a little girl started screaming yesterday morning while she was getting ready for school. Told her parents there was a dark man in her closet. And you can pretty much guess what her parents thought."

I nodded. I got it. "But they didn't find anything?"

"Nothing. They searched the house and after talking more with their daughter, she described the man as being made of dark stuff and wearing a hat."

"A hat?"

"Uh huh." The browser flipped again to another article. "This came in late last night. A guy was fighting with his wife and would probably have killed her. Except according to her, a whole bunch of little black ghosts came out of the television and surrounded him. She said it was like watching black ants swarm all over him."

"Did he make a comment?"

"Other than he was attacked by little black ghosts, no. And he was drunk so I don't think they were taking him seriously."

"So..." Kyle narrowed his eyes. "Two stories about ghosts brought you into work? Come on Ivan. One was a kid and the other a battered woman and drunk husband."

But Ivan wasn't going to be deterred. He gave Kyle a half smirk as he stared at him. The screen flipped again and stopped at another article.

I leaned in. "That's stamped today. This morning."

"Yes. This one's about a banker, getting ready for work. He went into his study to download his work from last night and saw something out of the corner of his eye. When he looked again, he swore he was saw a six foot shadow wearing a hat, standing by the room's closet where he keeps his old files and gold clubs. When he called out for his wife, it disappeared."

I straightened up. "How many of these did you find?"

"A half dozen. You see my point, right?"

Nodding, I pointed to the computer. "They're all local. All of those articles were written in *The Times - Picayune* with local writers."

"Right on it. I found about nine of them total. All of them talk about the same thing. Either a tall dark image of someone in a hat, or a bunch of smaller ones."

"Always a dark figure."

"Yep. And," he pointed to the shop phone. That's when I noticed the message light flashing. "When I called you guys and it went straight to voicemail, I decided to listen to messages to see if you'd been offline for a while. Maybe something was up. We've got three client messages, all of them being scared out of their mind when something either came out of their closet or out of the computer at them."

"What the hell?" Kyle immediately grabbed paper and pencil and started listening to the messages and writing them down.

"What are you getting at?" I asked him. "You're awfully excited about this."

"I think, and don't laugh," Ivan held up his hands. "But I think we're dealing with real, honest to Goddess, Shadow People!"

I wasn't laughing.

FIVE

"Shadow People?" I winced at him. "Who the hell are they?"

"Aw man…no way!" Ivan's grin was infectious. "You don't know about Shadow People? They're all over the Internet. Tons and tons of stories."

"I thought they were a myth? Like Slenderman?" Kyle said, the phone to his ear.

I looked at Kyle. "What's a Slenderman?"

"Sam…you really need to update your software." Ivan looked at the computer as a few new browser windows opened, all of them to websites about Shadow People. The last window to open was Wikipedia.

I pointed at it. "You do know that site is actually filled in by Internet know-it-alls."

"Yeah, and I wouldn't trust all of its information all the time. Which is why I start there and then do more research. See what it says up top?" He pointed to the screen.

Kyle finished taking some notes and glanced at the screen. "Yeah…" Kyle said. "And it's basically saying they're the perception of living shadow by supernatural nutcases." With his two cents in, he went back to listening to messages.

I laughed. The entry wasn't worded like that, but in essence, that's what it said.

Ivan wasn't deterred. "Ghost, spirits and entities are always, in truth, based on personal perception. Even we're defined by others' perceptions. There are still people on this Earth that think Witches ride on broomsticks and fornicate with the devil."

My mouth twisted to the side in a grumpy expression. I was inclined to believe that myself about a few acquaintances. "I get your point. But how are you putting this myth together with those articles?"

"Because they all have the same telling features." The browser windows shifted until a web page dedicated to Shadow People popped up. "There are at least five known types of Shadow People. And these local stories are specific to the tall ones with the hats, and the shorter, mischievous ones."

I stopped looking at the screen and refocused on Ivan. "So what are they?"

"No one knows. But all the stories point to them being malevolent."

Of course they are. I placed the thumb and middle finger of my right hand on my temples and squeezed. "Yeah, well…I'm not seeing anything that links this with the Elder deaths or anything relevant to what we have to do to appease the Clerics."

Ivan put a hand on my forearm and leaned in close to whisper. "If you want," he said in a low voice. "I can make something that would work. It would fool them—*owwhatthefuck?!*"

I jerked back just as Ivan did the same. He put a hand to his cheek and glared at my shoulder. "What?"

He pointed. "What the hell is that tucked in your hair?"

Tucked in my…*oh crap.* I directed a curious thought at the Sylph still hiding there and dismissed him with a thank you. "Sorry. I needed a witness."

"The little shit bit me."

I snickered as I redirected us back to the important offer he'd just made. "No…" He was thinking of uploading the book again and copying the information to make a new book, a perfect copy, to give to the Clerics. I put my hand on his shoulder as he leaned down again and I could see a tiny little bead of blood on his cheek. Yeah, that Sylph had taken a bite out of him. "You're a doll, Ivan. But we're not sure if your uploading and downloading is doing something else to you. These headaches worry me. And we don't have a witch doctor I can take you to who could diagnose if they're magic related or just physical stress."

He shrugged. "I say both. But I'm okay with trying it, just in case we have to."

Kyle put the receiver back in its cradle before he turned to us as I lowered my hand from Ivan's shoulder. "Sam, these Shadow People things may not have anything to do with what's happening with my aunt, but those articles Ivan found aren't an anomaly. I just jotted down information from ten messages."

"Ten?" Ivan whistled. "There were only three when I called in."

"Talk to me," I focused on Kyle.

"I wrote down the three Ivan mentioned, plus five more that all have the same ring to them."

"That only makes eight. What about the other two?"

"The other two are call backs from this particular message," he pointed to the paper in his hand. "This is a woman in the Garden District, not far from Ina's house. She said something flew out of the TV last night and attacked her dog. On her second call, she said her dog was acting funny. On the third call, her dog tried to kill her."

Oh shit. "Call her back. Get more information."

"You want to take this case?" Kyle picked up the receiver.

"What you just described sounds like a routine possession. Maybe a Fetch or a Daemon. It's something we can—"

All three of us jumped when someone banged heavily on the front door.

Arden Vervain, looking very southern stylish in her black couture suit and long leather coat, stood outside. She cupped her hands and pressed them to the window. Spotting us standing around the computer at the register, she waved. And yelled, "Hey! Kyle! Come on *shugar* and let me in. It's cold out here."

Ivan and Kyle looked at me. "You two go check out that lady's story. Call her back on your way there. If it is a possession—" I moved away from the counter and headed to the door.

"I'll kick it out on its ass," Kyle said.

"Go on! I need to talk to Arden."

"Got it," Kyle grabbed the edge of Ivan's hoodie. "Come on, Google boy. Let's go check this out and see if it's a possession. I'll drive."

Once they were safely through the door to the back, I unlocked the shop's front door and stood back. "Come in, Miss Vervain. It's been a while."

"Two weeks or so," Arden said as she entered the room. Arden Vervain didn't just walk into anything. She liked to make an entrance. "And I said to call me Arden."

I shut the door behind her. "Okay, Arden. I got a visit this morning."

"I'm sure you did. I got one too. So has everyone in the Elder Committee." She continued past the counter and into the back. I spotted Ivan's truck through the front windows as it moved down Bourbon Street toward St. Philip.

Arden was filling up the electric kettle when I came in. Grey sat on her big wolfie pillow by the door up to my apartment. The pillow was the kind they sold in pet stores for large dogs. Worked for her. As long as I kept it clean. "I like your wolf."

"What the hell, Arden?"

She glanced at me. Arden Vervain's age was a mystery to most people in New Orleans. She looked like she was in her mid-thirties, with brown hair that cascaded down broad but delicate shoulders. Her figure was something only seen in fashion magazines, as was her wardrobe. She was an Elder Witch, though she didn't possess three Dianic Gifts. Only one. But that one was a very unique and rare Gift. One of her Elemental Gifts was Water, which made sense when I thought of the swamp property she owned. And as a Dianic extra, Arden was a Seer.

And a very good one. She had an eighty-nine percent fruition rate. Best average in the country. The kicker was she didn't like using the Gift.

But it wasn't just her magic, or the fact she was a billionaire, that made people afraid of her. It was the control of her power that kept a lot of her enemies at bay. I'd seen Arden at work when she wanted to wield magic. Offensive or defensive—she had complete control. Most Witches had spells go wild, bend the wrong way and sometimes they just failed.

But not Arden.

She also had the power that comes with wealth. She really was the rich bitch who could get away with anything. And now the Clerics believed she murdered the Elders and they wanted her head.

I did *not* envy any of them in this situation.

The kettle started its boiling process as she lifted the tray with the sugar, cream and artificial sweetener to the table.

"Tea's in the cabinet."

"I know." Arden grabbed all seven boxes and put those on the table too. She set two large mugs beside the boxes and then stood by the kettle to wait on it. I think, in retrospect, that was the most mundane thing I'd ever seen her do. "Sam, I didn't kill those Elders."

"I honestly don't think you did." I pulled out a chair and sat. I figured if Arden Vervain was going to make me tea, I might as well enjoy it. Grey got up and came to sit beside me again and rested her head in my lap. I stroked her neck. "I don't see you as..."

"That stupid?" Arden waved her hand. "Those pricks do. I think sometimes they choose the most disreputable of us and give them to the office of Cleric just to get them off the streets."

"Could be." At least where Fred was concerned.

The kettle finished. Arden poured hot water into the two empty mugs and finally took a seat to my right. She picked out Earl Grey. I chose plain English breakfast and we steeped our bags. When it looked like Arden wasn't going to volunteer information, I prompted her. "Arden...they're going to submit a warlock ceremony to Parliament."

She pulled her tea bag up, and then let it go. "I know. I was informed of this myself. I'm being framed and I've never been framed for anything, or falsely accused."

"You're feeling helpless."

Now her dark eyes found mine. "Yes, I am. And I don't like it. This is not a state of being I wish to continue. The three Elders who died...I spoke with them on Sunday."

"At different times?"

"No. We had a meeting over at Ray's Cafe."

If I remembered correctly, that place had cameras. And I was pretty sure the cops already had surveillance. That is, if the NOPD knew about Arden. "That's not good."

"No. It's not. Witnesses. My card bill because I paid for it."

"Why did you meet?"

"It was a pitch session for me. I want the High Witch position. I'm not going to deny that. And those three Witches were instrumental in getting me elected as long as they bowed out of the race themselves."

"So everyone in the committee is up for election."

"Yes. Though a few have publicly said they didn't want the job. It's not a matter of choosing to run. As an Elder you have a responsibility."

I removed my tea bag and tossed it onto the condiments tray. The tray was an old classic Coca-Cola tin tray I found at a garage sale a few years back. The image was pretty much scratched off, but I liked the antique feel of it. "So you convinced them that you would be the best candidate." That was my assumption from their response on the emails.

"Nope." Arden did the same with her tea bag and then dumped two heaping tablespoons of sugar into it, stirred, and filled it to the brim with milk.

"You didn't convince them?"

"No. I was pretty much dismissed. We had a lovely meal and then they left. I sat there for a long time, imagining in my mind how each of them would meet their doom, but I didn't carry out anything."

I sipped my tea. "Do you know what the evidence against you is?"

"No." That got her attention. "Did they show you?"

"All three of the victims had typed out an email to you, agreeing that you were the best candidate."

Her eyes widened and for a second, Arden looked like a teenager who just learned her boyfriend was a woman. "All three of them…were typing out emails?"

"Weird, huh?"

"Yeah, *shugar*, it is. Why would they do that?"

I shook my head. "I have no idea. The Clerics are also convinced you have the Hammer."

Arden snorted. "They wished I had it. Damn old timers lost the thing and they want to blame me."

"You went into Higgins's house looking for it."

"I did."

"Twice."

Now she looked sheepish. "I wanted to make sure I had exhausted all my avenues."

"Arden," I sipped my tea again. "Is it possible Higgins hid the Hammer off campus?"

"Off campus?"

"Yeah. Like, not in his home?" The question was a total set up for me. I'd been thinking about Ivan's suggestion ever since he left, about making a copy of the book for the Clerics. I didn't want to put him through that again, but if they had their own copy, one that would fool a so-called Hammer expert, then it might be worth it. So putting the idea the Hammer could be somewhere in the city could give me the out I would need later.

At least if they had some copy of the damn thing, they'd leave me the hell alone. Or that was where my thoughts were going.

"I guess it's possible. If he believed it wouldn't be safe in his own home."

"Did you ever organize a search of the city?"

Arden sipped her tea. Then she took several large swallows. I assumed she was getting that sugar rush. "Not a very large search. But I can remedy that."

"Good. Now, let's get back to someone framing you and why." I leaned back in the chair as it creaked beneath me. Grey huffed and flopped down on the floor in a very good imitation of being bored. "I'm pretty sure if I told you to make a list of your enemies…"

"We'd be here for a year. Someone in my position always has enemies. My enemies have enemies *because* they're my enemies."

"You really need to learn to play well with others."

Arden shook her head. One short, curt shake. "It will never happen. And I've been racking my brain and yelling at my assistants all morning, trying to come up with someone that would love to see me not only incarcerated in the Cowen world, but in our world."

"They're the same world, Arden. Jail's jail."

"Not if you're warlocked."

True dat. "I don't know about DNA or the usual physical forensic anomalies that were found in their homes. But whoever did this knew the right evidence to leave. An email addressed to you in mid-creation works for the NOPD *and* the Clerics," I leaned my head onto my right shoulder. "Have the police come to question you?"

"Not yet. But I've left my assistants instructions to call me as soon as they show up. At either residence."

The fact the NOPD hadn't brought her in for questioning seemed odd to me.

My phone rang and vibrated in my back pocket. I leaned over just as Grey jumped up and loped into the front room.

My phone displayed the caller's face. Male, looked to be in his mid to late twenties, possibly early thirties. Chiseled features. Full lower lip on a mouth forever pulled to the side in a smirk. Long black lashes framed unusual amber red eyes. A thick shock of sandy brown hair flopped over his face, crowning shaved sides and back.

Detective Crwys Holliard.

My silent partner, former lover and unknown species.

"Yeah? Rent's not due for another two weeks."

Crwys laughed in my ear, but I could hear the tightness in his voice. "Miss Arden Vervain in there?"

"How did you guess?"

"This big-ass white limousine taking up half of Bourbon Street was my first clue," he sighed. "Come unlock the front door, Sam. I got a warrant for her arrest."

So much for odd.

SIX

Arden stepped into the front retail shop with me and remained by the counter as I unlocked the door. Crwys stepped in, squeezed my upper arm as he passed by. Detective Levi Tulouse, Crwys's partner, came in as well. Levi was rocking another of his crisp suits while Crwys wore his standard uniform of jeans, boots, t-shirt and leather jacket.

What I said earlier about Crwys being an unknown species wasn't a joke. I had a spell I called a *dex*, like a Pokédex, that would magically scan the Spirit of the person I directed it at and tell me what they were. Human, Fetch, Daemon, Revenant, Lamia and I recently added in Leviathan parameters.

When I used it on Crwys, and I used it a lot, it came up with no results. Not even a guess. I didn't know what he was, and he wasn't going to tell me. What I did know about him was that he was sexy as hell. My magic loved something about him and sometimes snapped me to him like a rubber band, and he could set people, places and things on fire.

Instantly. Poof. Gone. I'd recently watched him crispy-critter eleven Ghouls.

Levi, on the other hand, showed up with brilliant flares on my *dex*. Revenant. In other words, Vampire. But he seemed like a good guy. He caught the bad guys, and his demon, the thing in him that made him a Vampire, was named Ashur.

I know it gets confusing. But if you hang in there as long as I have, it starts to make a sort of chaotic sense.

Levi gave me a fist bump as he looked around the place. "Looks good in here, Sam."

I realized Levi hadn't been in since Dionysus's mad ninja Ghouls trashed the place. I wondered if he knew Crwys was one of my silent partners. I wouldn't be surprised if he did. He and Levi had been together a long time. A lot longer than playing cops and robbers as partners on the streets.

"Well, well, well, Detectives What and Vague. So nice to see you again."

Again? I looked at Crwys. He shrugged at me before he faced Arden. "You're not going to give us any trouble are you? 'Cause you know I love using my Witch mojo on you."

"That, *shugar*, could be misconstrued as a lewd and lascivious comment," she reached out and ran her long, red lacquered nail under his lightly bearded chin. "Do it again."

I didn't like her touching him.

Crwys wasn't mine. We weren't even a thing anymore. I was seeing Robin. Robin was mine.

But I still didn't like her touching Crwys. "So," I ventured and put a hand on Crwys's upper arm. That gesture disengaged his stare-down with Arden. "You're here to arrest Arden."

Arden's frown echoed my own. She moved her finger from Crwys's chin and pressed it against her own chest, just above her very visible cleavage. "Me? What can I do for you boys?"

Crwys's smile was a bit creepy. "You can turn around and put your hands behind your back." He held up a pair of handcuffs.

"Wait...you really are arresting her?" I looked from Crwys to Levi and back again. "Why?"

"Murder," Levi held up three fingers. "Three of them. Old white dudes. Not sure what she killed them with, but from the looks on their faces, it wasn't pretty."

Arden took a step back. I half expected her to summon a smoke cloud and do a classic disappearing act while she ran out the door and into her waiting car. When she didn't, I was a little proud of her.

A little.

"I haven't murdered anyone. I told you that yesterday."

"Turn around," Crwys took her upper arm and forced Arden to turn. "Hands behind your back."

Arden complied as Crwys slapped cuffs on her and Levi read her her rights. When they were done, I held up my hand. "Okay, so wait a minute. This has to do with the three dead Elders."

Crwys smiled at me. "I figured you'd know about that already."

"She only knows because I told her," Arden said. She turned to face us.

Crap. Even handcuffed Arden looked sexy. Having her hands pinned behind her just made her boobs stick out.

More.

"You might want to remain silent," Crwys warned.

"I told you. I had a meeting with them on Sunday. I did not kill them."

"DNA evidence says otherwise."

I blinked. "You got DNA evidence back—that fast? That's unbelievable."

"Not really," Levi said. "One of the stiffs is a friend of the chief of detectives. He's mad as hell the guy's dead so he's on the warpath."

"And next year is an election year," I muttered. "So you're arresting her on DNA evidence. What kind?"

"Sorry, Sam," Crwys took Arden's upper arm and sort of handed her off to Levi. "I think Frank's outside with a black and white. Just turn her over to him. Need to speak to Sam."

Levi looked suspicious, but he nodded.

Arden locked eyes with me and I nodded. "I'll look into it. I promise."

She mouthed the words "thank you" before Levi took her out the front of the shop.

"That was a pretty lousy way to do that. The tourists out there will see her."

Crwys was still watching the door as he shrugged. "Arden'll spin it to her own advantage. More publicity for her," he turned to face me. "Is Ivan around?"

"No. He and Kyle are out. Why do you need Ivan?"

"Got some questions to ask him, given his particular Gift," he took my arm and led me to a corner of the store as far away from the computer as possible and lowered his voice. "Do you guys know if he's the only one of his kind?"

"You mean a Cyber Witch?"

"Yeah. He ever run across others?"

I pursed my lips. "He's never said. Most of the stuff he can do is self taught, though recently he's been displaying a few more abilities."

"Like what?"

I shook my head. "Why are we whispering? There's no one in here but us."

Crwys's expression worried me. "Are you sure? Can your magic sense things that aren't there?"

"You mean like ghosts?" I searched his face, my gaze lingering on those red amber eyes. "You think a ghost is in my shop? There's no way, Crwys. I've got wards on wards to keep out the dead—"

He put a finger on my lips. Man, it was all I could do not to bite it. "Sshh. Just answer me. Do you have magic to detect invisible entities?"

"No. But I'm sure Kyle can make something," I narrowed my eyes at him. "You wanna tell me what this is about? Why are you talking about ghosts? And why arrest Arden when you know she didn't kill those Elders?"

"So you know they're Elders."

I sighed. "Because Arden *told* me. Weren't you listening? Or were you too focused on her boobs? That's why she was here. She wanted my help finding out who's framing her."

Crwys nodded slowly, but I got the feeling he wasn't really paying attention. "That's a good theory, but who said she was framed?"

"She did *not* kill those men."

"Can you be so sure?" he refocused on me. "How much do you really know about her? About her past? It's pretty colorful. She likes power. And from what I've gathered, those three were the only ones blocking her bid for High Witch."

"I know more about her than I know about you. And you expect me to trust *you*." A shadow passed along the back wall of the shop and I glanced at the front windows. The clouds were out and the only activity outside was a bunch of tourists taking pictures of the socialite in the back seat of the black and white cop cars.

Where had the shadow come from?

"Touché. But, do me a favor, ask Kyle to make something to detect things you can't see, okay? I'll pay him."

"You want a ghost detector."

"Yes," he raised his shoulders in an odd shrug. "More like a multi-planar dimensional detector."

"Crwys—"

"Say yes."

I sighed. "Yes."

He lowered his voice again. "Fingerprints were found on the keyboards they were writing those emails on too. And they all matched back to Arden Vervain."

"That's not DNA. That's fingerprints. And you and I know that kind of thing can be screwed up with magic."

"The DNA is going to come from hairs."

"Hairs? This is about hairs? She said she talked to them on Sunday. Had dinner with them. There is a logical explanation her hair might be on their jackets or something."

"These were in their underwear."

Well that stopped me. Also deadened any sexual desire I was feeling at that moment. The thought of Arden...ew. "Weren't these guys like, in their sixties?"

"Two were older," Crwys made a pained face. "Those tests they can't rush, so we're still waiting on the DNA."

"Meaning it might not be Arden's and you lied. She's going to make bail."

"Probably. Her lawyer's already at the station. Who else do you know with long dark hair and motive to silence three old men?"

I put my hand against the wall as another shadow moved over the opposite wall. Again, I looked out the window. No movement, other than Levi smoking a cigarette.

"Why do you keep looking at the wall?"

"Not sure," I said as I stepped away from him and walked around the shop. I held out my right hand and called up a small white sphere made of Spirit. It was by definition, an extension of my own. It lifted up and moved around the room like a sensor, looking into every corner and crevice of the shop.

When it came near the computer, the feedback from it felt like knives slicing down my back. I dismissed it immediately and the pain stopped. I'd put my hands to my head and pressed my palms over my eyes.

"Sam? Baby please...look at me."

Baby?

That was the gentlest tone I'd heard Crwys use with me since we broke off the relationship. I opened my eyes and looked up at him through my fingers. He had his hands on my shoulders and he was very, very close. Every magical thread in my body inched toward him. The blood that made me what I was demanded him.

My breathing hitched and I put my hands on his chest. He was breathing hard as well and we were in the middle of the shop now, almost arm in arm.

"You're....you're an Incubus, aren't you?"

He laughed. "No. I'm not. We met one of those, remember?"

I smiled at him. "Yeah, we did."

Someone knocked on the front door. Loud.

We both turned to see Levi visible through the window. He pointed to his watch.

"I gotta go," Crwys disengaged and my body instantly cooled.

Well, if he wasn't an Incubus, he sure as hell should be. I took in a few deep breaths but I was gonna have a headache.

"Sam, if you come up with anything in your case with Arden, let me know?"

I didn't say a word, nor did I nod or shake my head as I watched him leave. He and Levi got into Crwys's Mustang and pulled away, the black and white carrying Arden, long gone.

The hairs on the back of my neck stood on end. This was never a good sign. I pivoted slowly to look behind me just as I heard Grey growling low in her throat. I tiptoed through my shop, looking around bookcases and tables to find my wolf and see what she was growling at.

I was unnerved when I saw her backside sticking out from behind the counter in the back. "Hey girl...you sense something creepy too?"

She didn't stop growling as I came around. She was low on her front paws, her lips pulled back and all kinds of teeth showing. Her gaze was fixed on the corner of the shop where the computer was.

Where Ivan usually sat.

I immediately summoned my *dex*. White pentagrams appeared in various shapes then switched colors as they took up the Elements to summon Spirit. They spun and rocked in the air between Grey and I and the computer area.

Nothing.

Not a damn thing came up.

My phone rang. I yelled out. The pentagrams vanished and Grey barked.

My heart was in my throat as I fumbled at my back pocket. Sweet Lady...that scared the crap out of me. I finally got the damn thing out, cursing the whole time how Ivan's presence made electronic devices possible, and looked at the phone's face.

I paused.

That wasn't a name I expected to see.

Pauline Hawthorne.

My stepmother.

I thought about sending it to voicemail. But I'd done that for the past three months; avoiding the guilt she was going to lay down on me. When the shop's name showed up in the local papers for vandalism she called every day for a week after that.

Mom disappeared when I was eight. No one really explained to me what happened, just that she was killed. The cover answer had always been she was working undercover—she was a homicide detective—and the job took her away. The truth had been much darker.

She'd been an Elemental Witch like me, and she was her coven's Tracker as well as the district's, as I learned later. She'd been after what

I discovered was a Leviathan, a creature much like a Revenant (they were from the same family). Revenants were made when the possessing demon was invited in to share the body. Leviathans took bodies, used them, and often times rode the host souls like slaves. So when the body took damage, the soul felt it, not the Leviathan.

This particular Leviathan, whose demon's name was Dionysus, tracked my mother down and made a deal with the Obsidian Queen of the Faeries, Medbh, to kill my mother in exchange for the Leviathan's host soul. Medbh did take my mother, but Dionysus skipped hosts in her plan to cheat the queen. He took refuge inside my mother's best friend, the Witch who tried to complete the Arcane spell that would exorcise Dionysus and send him back to the Well of Souls.

Without my mother, the spell failed. And Inamorata Devonshire became a Leviathan.

But the story didn't end there. No…Medbh found Dionysus and took the soul, fusing the Leviathan to the host body. Dionysus hid in plain sight after that for eighteen years.

As my aunt. She moved in with my dad and took care of me. Taught me magic and I had no idea that the reason I didn't have my mother was tucking me into my bed at night. Dionysus was biding her time until the opportunity came to reverse the Faerie Queen's deal and take another soul. It was just magic justice that I ended up in possession of that same Faerie's head nearly two decades later.

But when I turned twelve my dad met Pauline Willbanks. They fell in love and I thought she was good for him. She didn't get along with Ina and gave my dad an ultimatum. Choose one or the other.

Dad chose Pauline. And Ina convinced me that I was better off living with her so that she could continue teaching me magic and my dad would have the chance of a normal life.

Then a few weeks ago, I learned that truth. I killed an innocent. And Dionysus got that poor girl's soul.

And now, thinking back on it, I wondered if dad knew the truth all along about why mom disappeared. I thought about visiting him and asking him about that time. That night. I wanted to pick through his memories.

49

But that just wasn't possible anymore.

Because George Hawthorne had been diagnosed with dementia a year ago and it was a rare day when he knew who I was.

SEVEN

"Hello Pauline," I said as I leaned against the register counter. I wasn't completely over my little ghost scare and Grey looked like she was still watching Ivan's computer. Crwys's ghost spell request wasn't helping my mood either. "How's it going?"

"Well I'll be," came the surprised response. Pauline was a kind woman, a retired nurse and a Godsend when it came to handling dad these days. "You actually exist."

I ignored the barb. "Yes. I've been busy."

"I'll say. You fix things after that vandalism? Those cops in New Orleans find those wretched people?" Pauline had a very southern accent, something that wasn't exactly Mississippi or Louisiana, but more mid-Georgia.

"Yes ma'am. They caught them. Everything's fine," I kept looking at the computer and at the corner as I put my free hand on Grey's neck. "What's up, Polly? Why did you call?"

"Oh Sam, it's your father."

"What…he didn't run away again did he?" To say dad *ran away* was a little funny to me. The truth was he tended to start out on an afternoon walk and just kept going. "Did he mess with the hospice nurse again?"

"No, Adelaide doesn't work with us anymore. She complained about him and vice versa. New nurse is named Robbie. She's a doll. I like her a lot," Polly paused and I stopped petting Grey. "This is something else."

"It's his condition, isn't it? It's gotten worse?"

"I can't tell. He's started talking to the wall in the den."

I blinked a few times, trying to digest that as the door opened and a customer came in. She was tall and well endowed and waved at me like she knew me. I smiled and made sure she saw I was on the phone. Yeah, I know, it was rude for a store owner to be on the phone while a customer was around, but…eh…screw it. "What exactly does that mean?"

"It means he's in his chair facing away—the one by the fire—and he's talking away to the corner where the computer sits. Just having a conversation. I mentioned it to the doctor, but he seemed to think it was normal. I don't. He's never done that before."

"Polly, it is dementia."

"I'm a retired nurse, Samantha, I know what dementia is. But I also know every patient is different and it effects people differently. I might be a bit more forgiving of the doc's assessment, except…"

I kept an eye on the customer as I moved behind the counter, in case she wanted to buy something. "Polly…except what?"

"Yesterday, George was talking to the wall and it was like an argument. He started yelling and shouting. I was in the kitchen making us lunch. I heard something crash so I ran in and found him hurling things at that same corner. He busted three of those antique vases on the shelf."

Now I had a better idea in my head what part of the den he was talking to. Polly's computer was in the farthest corner, in the nook where mom and dad once had matching chairs. It was where they liked to unwind and talk at the end of the day.

But even though I knew in what direction he was hurling things, the panic my dad might be becoming manic in some way and could hurt Polly kicked in. "Is he okay? Are you okay? He didn't try to hit you, did he?"

"No. He didn't. But he…when I took the last vase from him and told him to calm down, he grabbed my arm and said…" Polly breathed into the phone. "Sam, he said I had to call you."

"Call…me?"

"His exact words were, call Sam. She's got to come and exorcise her mother."

The woman browsing the small, engraved stones in the far corner made a strange movement with her hand. I reached out with a few of what I called my *feels*, extensions of me that could sense and sort of "see" things. Like what she just put in her pocket.

It was a small stone, engraved with the word Laugh on it. It was all of three bucks, and this chick was going to shoplift? I pulled on the strings of those *feels*, willed a bit of Earth down the connection—specific to rock—and launched that rock right out of her pocket so it landed a few feet from the door.

The woman looked startled when the rock made a noise on the hardwood floor and looked at me with a confused look on her face. I smiled and waved goodbye as she left the shop.

Probably going to think the place is haunted now. And with that thought, Medbh came to mind. Though she'd been a pain in the ass since I brought her home, she *had* given the place a sort of atmosphere with her sporadic giggling and singing. And yeah, everyone heard her.

"Sam?"

"Sorry. I had a customer." I refocused on what my dad had said. Dad knew, *had* known that is, that I was a Witch. He'd knowingly married one. So calling for me to get rid of a ghost was actual, cognitive thinking. The fact he was *talking* to a ghost or could possibly *see* one well enough to throw things at it? That was a little frightening. I mean was it real considering what had been happening all morning on my end? Or was it the dementia? How did you know?

Him saying the ghost was my mom both intrigued and irritated me. I didn't really know that much about ghosts. I hadn't met many over the years and usually I'd been able to explain hauntings logically. Magnetic fields, noisy pipes and the usual over active imagination.

"Polly...you're a nurse. Do you think he's really seeing something?"

Her laugh caught me off guard. And then I remembered Pauline didn't know anything about me, about what I was, or what my mother had been. "I think he thinks he's seeing something in his mind. That's dementia. Whatever is going on, I'm sort of reluctant to take him to the doctor."

"You think they'll want him in a home."

"Yeah. He was throwing things, Sam. And when they start getting violent, doctors usually like them in a facility where that can be addressed."

I knew what that meant. Addressed meaning they could dope him up to make him non-violent.

That bruised my heart knowing my dad had never been violent in his life. This was the same man who used to capture spiders in the house to take them outside before me or Ina stomped them.

I don't like spiders.

But Dad? He loved everything.

"You think me coming to see him might help?"

"That's what I'm hoping."

Yeah, I could see that. She and Dad still lived in Picayune, which was just over an hour drive from New Orleans. The problem was everything going on in my life, especially and most importantly, dealing with that threat of Arden's warlocking by Cleric assholes. I checked the clock over the door. The boys had been gone a long time, and I was getting hungry. I was also feeling like the entire world had taken up residence on my shoulders. "Polly, I understand. But there's no way I can get there this week. You think he'll hold out till maybe next Wednesday?" That gave me about four days to clear all this bullshit up, and hopefully clear Arden's name.

She didn't answer at first and I could feel her disappointment through the phone. "Yeah. If he asks again, I'll tell him you're getting here as fast as you can."

"Thanks Polly. I'm sorry. It's just crazy here."

"It's New Orleans, Sammie..." Polly said as she laughed. It sounded hollow. "It's always crazy."

We hung up and I pulled Ivan's stool from the creepy corner and sat on it. I really did feel the weight of everything at that moment. Mine and Robin's increasing arguments, the stress of worrying if my use of Arcane was going to manifest somehow into something horrible, the truth about Arwen's death I hid from everyone, Arden's request for help to find who was framing her, the warlock threat which now depended on me finding their damn Hammer, and now my dad.

Was his dementia getting that bad? I didn't know. I was ashamed I hadn't kept up with him, or Polly. I had been too involved in my own drama to take a peek outside of my own world.

What really sucked about it all was that usually when I started feeling like this, I went to Ina.

But Ina didn't exist. She'd never been real. To me.

And now she was gone, somewhere in the world. I hated to think Dionysus would abandon that body somewhere and leave it to rot alone. Inamorata had been my mom's closest friend. She didn't deserve to have her life taken like that. The only comfort I had was knowing Medbh took her soul and returned it to the Well before Dionysus could abuse it.

I wiped at my cheek and looked down at the beautiful face looking up at me. Grey whined a few times and I leaned forward to kiss the top of her head. "Just having a little pity party, girl. Not sure where to turn. I need to talk to someone, but it can't be Ina."

Grey woofed.

"Yeah, and I just can't talk to Crwys."

Grey's ears twitched back then forward, almost in a question.

"Because he confuses me. It's bad enough he's part owner of this place now. Not to mention every time I see him I want to take my clothes off."

Grey growled low in her throat.

I laughed at her. "I'm not falling into that trap again. Not till I know exactly what it is I'm sleeping *with*," I cringed after I said that. It was just wrong.

Maybe it was time to start confiding in Kyle and Ivan. They were a large part of my life now, and though they we were both around the same age as me; I always saw them as much younger and in need of mothering. Eh…had to be that Elemental nature of mine.

I retrieved my phone and pressed the button.

But instead of my usual locked screen of a full moon, a shadow looked back at me. I was so startled I dropped the phone and jumped back. The stool fell backward and Grey took off across the room, startled.

It wasn't often I was frightened like that. I'd seen a lot of crap in my life, sometimes to a point where what scared the average person barely made a blip on my radar. But that...

I tried recalling exactly what I'd seen from my memory—and that's where it got hard. There weren't any real distinguishing features to it. Just the impression of a face, with sunken holes for eyes and tiny red dots. I couldn't remember a mouth or even a nose.

Grey returned looking a little embarrassed that she ran away. She bent her nose at the phone. It landed with the face on the floor, which of course, just made the idea of picking it up and turning it over to see the face again a bit more scary.

I watched her sniff it, and then she wagged her tail. I took that as a sign and retrieved it.

When I turned it over, I gasped.

A crack moved from the lower left corner all the way up to the upper right corner. I stared at the crack for a while as Grey whined at me. At first I thought...I could have sworn...I saw a thin, red worm crawling out from the crack across the glass. Then another one popped out.

More of the red worms poured out from the crack and squirmed around on top of the glass. I recognized what I was seeing—this was Ivan's description of what he saw when he viewed Arcane Magic. Usually, I saw it as red and sparkling. Like glitter.

The smell followed the worms. The rotting chicken aroma.

Grey barked.

The phone buzzed, and then rang as Crwys's number showed up. I slammed the phone on the counter. The worms abruptly disappeared. There was no way I was answering that.

I ran my fingers through my hair. I needed to find my center and think. Times like this, I wished I had a bunch of whiteboards I could throw up in my apartment and just write everything down like a detective would. Put all the tiny pieces together and look at things in a whole instead of feeling overwhelmed by a dozen little things.

Though my dad losing his mind and me being threatened with being warlocked weren't *little* things.

Ina had whiteboards in her house. She used to use them to teach students.

Well, she used them to teach her Ghouls how to kill people and do her bidding. But they were still whiteboards. As far as I knew, no one had been in the house since the night I killed Arwen and ended up in the hospital. My hand went to the spot on my neck where Dionysus bit me.

The house was legally mine. Ina—Dionysus—had insisted on us jointly owning it. I never understood why. He was gone. Crwys suspected he was off starting a new life, probably one he'd been planning on for a while. Might have even taken a new body. Probably a man this time.

Me? I wasn't so sure. Dionysus had invested a lot of time taking care of me—but I didn't know why. Me. The daughter of his tormentor. I had this bad suspicion I wasn't going to find that out for a while, and when I did, I wasn't going to like it.

Going back into that house wasn't my top priority. But I needed to be away from everyone for a breather. How was I going to react emotionally to returning to a house where I murdered someone?

I didn't know. But if there was one thing Dionysus had taught me, it was to face my fears head on. Don't run from them, but run into them.

And right now, I was afraid of that house. Of what I did. And that fear had kept me in a state of hesitancy for the past two weeks. I felt if I moved through this level, I could think clearer and pick a direction.

Any freak'n direction.

I grabbed my phone with a dishtowel, even though I didn't see anymore of those little red worms, slipped it into my bag, grabbed my guns and loaded Grey in the Jeep.

It was time to face fear number one head on.

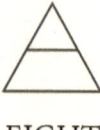

EIGHT

The smell that hit me when I opened the door knocked me back a few steps. Grey whined but she went inside. It wasn't like a garbage smell. More like an earthy, compost heap smell. And I had a pretty good idea where it came from.

I learned about Dionysus's plan for my mom and Ina's unwilling part in it all on Halloween. Ina had been in the kitchen making pies and the center island had been filled with baskets of all sorts of apples. Granny Smith, Fuji, Pink Ladies, MacIntosh…

Now, all of those apples were little more than rotted husks in ruined baskets in the kitchen. The pies she'd made sat on the stove where she'd put them to cool and each one was covered in a thick, green mold.

I stood by the island looking down at the place where Dionysus tried to drain me. My blood, now stained brown, still coated parts of the white tile floor. There weren't any black dusts of powder where a CSI team looked for prints. No police tape in the back yard around the Circle.

Because Crwys had taken care of everything. There was no body to find. No evidence of what I'd done. Except what I held in my memory and the sparkle of glittering red I sometimes saw when I worked magic. It was small, just a tinge of it, but it was there.

Arcane.

It was permeating my magic. Slow but steady. Was this what it was supposed to do? Everything I'd ever been told about Arcane Magic was that it was forbidden, that it was evil and it would destroy a Witch's soul. And I guess it had destroyed mine in a way. I'd been so focused on thinking Arwen was the Leviathan I was looking for that I couldn't see the reality in front of me.

Something moved out of my peripheral vision. It was fast and low, and I thought for a second it was Grey, but she was at my feet. She was looking in the same direction, her ears perked forward.

The motion had been in the dining room just off the kitchen. I summoned a Salamander as my hand burst into red flame and moved cautiously into that room. The Salamander hovered nearby, watching the room too, and turned as if watching something move past it.

"Is there someone here?" My voice did nothing to reassure me. It was possible there were transients, or homeless kids in the house. Dionysus had usually opened this house to them, and now I shuddered thinking of what he might have done to them right under my nose.

The Salamander turned to me and shrugged. I dismissed him with a thank you and cautiously moved through the rest of the lower level. Nobody but me.

I put my hands to my face and took a deep breath. All this talk about ghosts, Shadow People and Crwys wanting a *Ghostbusters* Spell was making me jumpy. It didn't help that my own dad wanted me to exorcise Mom. The best thing to do would be clean it all up. Wash it away. And *cleanse* the house.

Get rid of all traces of Dionysus.

Grabbing gloves out of the broom closet, I cleared the kitchen of all its rotten apples, the baskets, the moldy pies and what was still in the oven. The ovens were off. I assumed Crwys had shut them off so they wouldn't start a fire and bring attention to this house.

Once everything was bagged, I ran hot water into a bucket and mopped with every detergent I could find, including bleach.

Never dismiss the magic of bleach.

I'd been in the house a little over two hours by the time I finished cleaning the kitchen and the dining area. The rest of the house looked like it always had. The herb room was the saddest to me. Most of Ina's potted plants were brown and dying from neglect. I watered what I thought could be saved and threw out the rest.

After sweeping dead leaves from the floor, I moved on to Ina's room upstairs—everything looked as if the owner had just stepped out to the store. As if life had been cut off. I looked through her clothing, the drawers, a chest—anything I thought she'd leave some kind of clue as to where she went.

Nothing.

Until I took a long look at the mirror. I wasn't looking at myself, but more at the glass. There was something smudged there, reflected in the afternoon light coming through the bedroom window. Someone wrote something on the mirror.

I narrowed my eyes at it, bent forward, took a deep breath and then breathed on the glass. Not like a regular breath, but a mouth open breath, like most people did when they wanted to polish or buff something.

When I stepped back, a message appeared.

The box is yours.

The box? I looked around the room. There were a lot of boxes, but nothing I could designate as mine. I examined the dresser where the note was written and spotted a small, blue dust-covered box behind a picture of me and Ina when I was fourteen and we moved into this new house.

I picked the box up and my fingers tingled. Was this a booby-trap? Something that was going to hurt me physically or magically? I held the box in my left hand and waved my right over it. A white pentagram spun into being and passed around the box. Nothing flagged. No alarm.

Grey padded into the room and whined. I lowered the box for her to see it and she touched it with her nose.

"I guess it means it's okay." But I was very suspicious of anything left here by Dionysus.

Inside was a delicate silver pentagram. I carefully held it out to get a good look at it in the light. Around the circle and woven into the crossing bars that made the star was the etched image of a tree.

I recognized it immediately. This was the symbol my mom's

coven had used when I was a kid. All the members had one of these, and I had wanted one myself. But I had to be initiated first.

Was this Inamorata's pentagram? Her sigil from the coven before Dionysus took her?

Balancing it in my hand, I lowered it to Grey again. "Whatcha think, girl? Should I wear it?"

Grey put her nose into my palm and backed up, moving her head from side to side. I was gonna take that as a no. And I agreed. Jewelry from Dionysus was a bad idea, seeing as how he'd given me that heirloom necklace with the ability to suck souls into it.

I put the pentagram back in the box and back on the dresser. "No thanks, asshole. If I wore one, it'd be my mom's."

Grey barked and the hairs on the backs of my arms stood on end. Looking in the mirror, I saw something in the bed behind me. I whirled with my hands up, white fire ready.

But there was nothing there. No one else in the room.

The Circle was visible from the window overlooking the back garden. From the second story, everything looked peaceful. Quiet. Nothing there to tell the tale of what happened in the Sacred Space.

"Come on girl. Time for me to face the music."

But once in the garden, and in the center of the Circle, standing in the very spot where Arwen died—there was nothing to face. No music. Not a sound. It was a dead zone. No hint of power, no thrill to touch the edges of my soul.

The ground glittered red where I shed her blood, and I had to keep telling myself that was Arcane and not real blood. Real blood was long gone, either by Crwys's hand or by that of nature.

When I stepped away from that space, I could feel the Circle again.

I'd left a dead zone in the center of Sacred Space. This had also been the place where I'd talked to Tzariene, the Seelie Queen, also known as the Silver Queen of Faerie. The Summer Court.

Maybe if I cleansed the Circle and was able to talk to Tzariene again, I could find out if the original children were in *Alfheim*. If I could find them, that would be at least one thing off my list of things to make right.

The Silver Queen would need something in trade. We'd used honey milk before. I'd have to think on an appropriate trade later. I had to clean up my mess first.

Searching through Ina's books, I didn't come up with anything, and several times while in her library I got the feeling I was being watched. But when I looked up—there was nothing there. My nerves were shot.

Eventually, I came to the assumption that the only way to cleanse Arcane was with an Arcane spell. Back in the kitchen I removed the necklace and pulled the drive from its chain. After setting it on the now clean center isle, I put my hand on the drive and said, "Open sesame."

The drive instantly expanded in a beautiful, swirling sparkle of red glitter. I stepped back as it pulled more Arcane from the air itself, and from my fingertips. It started unfolding and unfolding until it was the proper size with the last bend and became a book.

Grey growled and I waved at her to shush. She didn't like the book, and she'd tried to chew it up a few times.

To anyone else but Ivan and I, this book would look like a copy of the Malleus Maleficarum. Hardback. Old leather cover.

To us it was a spell book of Arcane Magic, and the very book the Clerics had threatened me for that morning.

Had it only been just this morning?

The problem with books like this was the lack of an index. I'd seen a big spell book once that actually had one, and a table of contents, but that book wasn't accessible as it was in Savannah, Georgia.

So I had to go through it page by page.

A loud noise startled us. Grey jumped up from where she'd been lounging on the kitchen floor and ran into the dining room. Again.

I dove into my bag by the stove and retrieved my guns. With the Lady in my left and the Lord in my right, both of them loaded and ready to fire, I pressed my back to the wall on the kitchen side of the archway. On the count of three I turned with both hands out, both guns up and ready.

Before, when I summoned the Salamander, I'd been thinking of having to deal with supernatural elements. Things that were Arcane and magic based. But the slam and footsteps I was hearing now were made in the physical world, so I was now thinking I was dealing with an intruder. A real one, and not my imagination.

As I moved through the dining room I glanced through the sliding glass door to the Circle—

Someone was moving inside at the Circle! Well son of a bitch! Someone had broken into Ina's backyard, which as far as I knew, was impossible. I ran to the door, opened it and moved along the tall cypress I'd helped Ina plant when we moved into the house.

"Freeze!" I shouted as I burst through and pointed my guns at the altar.

The person I'd seen wasn't there. No one was there.

I heard another noise, this time from inside the house and Grey was howling, barking, and growling.

I ran back to the house, burst through the door and saw the back of Grey in the doorway to the kitchen. But just as I arrived and pointed my guns inside, I saw…

It.

There was no other way to describe it. It wasn't a man or a woman that I could see. It was close to six feet tall and made of…shadow.

It was the image of someone, but not the substance. And it was bending over the Hammer.

"You hold it right there, asshole."

The thing did seem to hesitate before it turned and looked at me. It had eyes…and a nose…just like the thing in my phone had.

A deep, low and slow laugh that reminded me of the Uncola 7UP guy, vibrated the tile floor under my feet as it bowed to me, just before it plunged its hands into the book.

I fired over and over again, but the bullets went through it and struck the range hood, the fridge, the doorframe to the TV room and the island itself.

The laughter increased in volume as it, and the book, did this weird motion blur and vanished.

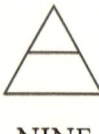

NINE

I ran to the island and slapped both of my hands, with the guns, on the counter.

No!

I put the guns on the island and bent down to look under it. I ran into the TV room, the living room and the herb room. But the shadow form and the book were gone.

My phone rang in the bag and it took me a minute to figure out where it was. I remembered the red worms and hesitated as I pulled it out. The crack was still there but the worms were gone. Kyle was calling so I put him on speakerphone 'cause I really, really needed to talk to him. "Hey, you're not going to believe what just happened—"

"I'm pretty sure I will, 'cause you need to sit down."

I put the phone on the island as I continued looking around. That thing took the Hammer! And this bit of knowledge was causing me no end of panic. Without that book, Ivan couldn't make a copy. Without a copy to give to the Clerics, they were going to try and warlock Arden and she was going to blame me if that happened. "I am not sitting down!" I yelled at the phone, and realized I had a bit of hysteria in my voice.

"Okay then stand. That first house with the dog? You were right. Just a simple Daemon. Kicked that out with a spell. The other stuff? Sam…these things are real. Ivan and I both saw them."

"What things? Ghosts?"

"No, these Shadow People."

I straightened up. Right…the people Ivan talked about. "What did they look like?"

"They're sort of different sizes, but none are as tall as Ivan and I. And they're fast. It's easier to look at them if you sort of try to out of the corner of your eye. You can't really see them if you look at them head on."

I knew for a fact that wasn't completely true. "Ah…you said they were shorter than you two?"

"Yeah. Even shorter than you."

I wasn't that short. I was 5'7".

"But do they have arms and legs and red pinpoint eyes?"

"Eyes? No…uh uh. No eyes. But they do have arms and legs. And they laugh. A lot. Ivan swears he can hear them crying."

The laughter….check. I put my hand flat on the island's surface where the book had been. "I think I just saw one too. Only mine was over six foot and it had a laugh like the Uncola guy."

I heard Kyle talking to someone whom I assumed was Ivan. A pause and then Ivan's voice came through. "Tell me what you saw, Sam."

I described it as best I could, and I also told him about seeing the same kind of face on my phone. And the worms.

Ivan didn't say anything at first, then. "You saw that thing on your phone?"

"Yeah. It looked like it was in my phone looking out at me."

"Where are you?"

"I'm at Ina's house."

Another pause. "Why are you there?"

I sighed. "Long story. Just…am I on speaker?"

"Yeah."

"Take me off."

He did and I could tell because the background noise shut off. "Hold on," Ivan said and then finally. "Sam, what's wrong?"

"It took the Hammer, Ivan."

"It…what?"

"The Shadow Guy I saw took the damn Hammer."

"From around your neck?"

I gave him a very, very brief run down of what I was going to do, without going into details or telling him about my cleaning spree. Ivan didn't say anything at first. "And you're sure it's gone."

"Ivan…the damn thing is gone. I watched it put its hands on it and it blurred and vanished."

"It blurred. That meant it was traveling, so it's not there anymore. But how did it get into Ina's house? That place is like, super uber warded."

"You don't think the thing on my phone was the same as this, do you?"

When Ivan didn't answer, I groaned out loud. "Ivan, I've got to get that book back."

"It can't use the book, Sam. So there's no issue there. And it was a bad book anyway."

"Remember what you overheard this morning?"

"Yeah…oh…fuck…"

"Now you see why I'm panicking," I picked the phone up and carried it with me to the herb room. "This can't be a coincidence."

"It's not. I'm going to text you an address. You need to get here. 'Cause I think Kyle might have something you need to hear."

After transferring the texted address into my GPS, I loaded my stuff and Grey back into the Jeep and headed toward this house. The address put it on Dante Street near Riverbend, which was an area I wasn't familiar with so I needed to follow the route.

My phone rang in the middle of me programming the route. It was Pauline's number so I ignored the call and pushed it to voicemail.

And of course, Robin called once I was on my way. I answered him but kept him on speaker as I drove. "Hey Robin. I'm on the road. Can I call you back—"

"I saw Kathy! Sam…I saw Kathy!"

I slowed the Jeep down for a red light. "Robin, Kathy's dead."

"No, Sam. She's here. In the house. Rose's house. I was cleaning out some of Rose's things and she was there in the corner and she tried to talk to me."

I bowed my head until my forehead banged the steering wheel. Now Robin was seeing ghosts. Which was absurd because I doubted wherever Kathy was, and I suspected it was *Alfheim*, she was going to show up as a ghost. She wasn't going to show up at all. So either Robin was going nuts, or there was something playing tricks on him. "Baby… describe what you saw."

He did.

A car horn startled me and I hit the gas to go forward, not realizing the light had turned green.

"Sam, you there? Can you come over and see her for yourself?"

I looked at the map on the phone. I was close to Rose's house and it was going to take another half hour to get over to Riverbend. I was terrified something awful was happening to Robin now that I had my dad's dementia on my mind. I pulled to the right and took a side road as the GPS started recalculating. I reached up and stopped it. "I'll be there in a few minutes, baby."

"Thank you Sam. I knew you'd understand. I love you."

"I love you too." I heard him disconnect and I white-knuckled the steering wheel all the way to Rose's house.

TEN

The sun was in my eyes as I pulled into Rose's driveway. The black wreath still hung on the door as I got out and Grey followed me up the walk. Robin met us at the door and ushered us inside. I'd been to Rose's house a few times, when she was alive and a single mother of two. The other daughter was with Robin's parents while Robin volunteered to pack up the house.

From the looks of things, and the smell, Robin hadn't been doing a lot of either. He looked even more haggard than he had that morning at *Bell, Book and Candle*. He put a hand on my back and sort of half coaxed and half pushed me into the den.

The house was a single level with a formal front room and then a hall to the left to the kitchen and a den/dining room area with a fireplace. A see-through counter separated the den from the kitchen.

No fire burned in the hearth, which seemed odd to me since Rose always kept it burning in the winter. She told me once how the house always seemed so cold to her. I wondered in a sad way if she was still cold in death.

Discarded pizza boxes, Chinese take out cartons and tin Mexican food containers littered the coffee table, the counter, a side chair and spilled out of the garbage can. I thought after Robin and I left the hospital two weeks ago, he would need my help to get him through the two deaths. But after a few days of silent lunches and awkward dinners, I stopped calling.

So did he.

It wasn't until this morning I really understood how much he blamed himself and how much his family blamed him as well. I didn't have magic to fix this. Robin had acted in self-defense, and no matter what he or anyone else thought, he hadn't killed his niece.

"Sam, if you sit right here on the couch beside me…and can Grey stay outside? I don't think she'll come if there's a dog in the house."

Grey woofed. I knew she didn't like being called a dog. No respectable wolf would, I assumed. I looked at her. She rolled her eyes and lumbered to the back door on the den side of the counter as Robin opened the door. "It's okay. The back's fenced in so she won't run."

I knew she wouldn't run. So did Grey. And I could almost feel her sitting just outside that door.

I sat as Robin directed me and he sat beside me and laced his fingers with mine. We faced the fireplace for a few minutes. My phone rang in my pocket but I ignored it.

After a few awkward moments I finally said, "Robin—"

"Just wait, please? She wanted me to get you to come."

I turned my head to the right to look at his handsome profile. "She said that to you?"

"Not in so many words. It was more of a feeling. Every time I watched her, I thought of you."

That didn't sound good. It certainly wasn't ghostly communication and usually when things wanted me, it was to kill me or stop me from exorcising their ass back to where they belonged.

But, like I said, I didn't know a lot about ghosts.

I squeezed his hand and watched the fireplace. My phone went off again. It was Pauline. I hit ignore again. Several minutes went by before I opened my mouth to say something.

That's when I caught a movement inside the darkened fireplace. My brain kicked in, and my Witchy curiosity with it, as I noticed, for the first time, how dark the fireplace was. I had one of these brick jobs in the apartment above my shop, and it was never that dark and almost cavernous inside.

Something moved again and I focused on it. Not directly but sort of out of the corner of my eye.

As it moved a third time, I took copious mental notes on how it was moving, what it looked like and how ruddy scared I was.

It had a head, a body, two arms and two legs, but that was it. It really looked like a shade or a shadow of someone cast on the ground by bright sunlight. But there was no one there to cast anything. It moved painstakingly slow, as if it was having trouble. It jerked and then flashed, as if a film had frames taken out, as it stepped out of the fireplace and stood in front of it.

My jaw dropped to my chest. I was sitting there watching a walking shadow shuffle within the space in front of the fireplace. It tilted its head and I had the impression it was looking at Robin. Though I'm using *looking* as a very loose term.

I moved my gaze from it to Robin. His face was euphoric, his eyes glazed and his mouth parted as if asleep. The thing took another jerky step around the coffee table toward him and this time I reacted. I thought I'd seen something between them. Some kind of strange ghosty, wispy lines.

When I moved forward on the couch the thing hesitated, and then started toward Robin again. Grey began barking and growling behind the door. The hairs on my arms went up like they had in Ina's house just before I saw that thing in the kitchen. I stood up and moved between this shadowy creature and Robin.

The thing elongated and thinned out until it towered over me. Glowing red eyes popped out of its darkness as the shadowy substance split under them and a mouth opened and snarled at me.

I saw teeth.

Shiny, metallic teeth in the shadow.

"Aw, no you don't," I said as I called all four Elements and formed a barricade around Robin. The four Elementals appeared in their forms. My favorite Salamander, the Sylph from before, an Undine, and a Gnome the size of a Hobbit landing with firm feet on the ground. She had an axe with her and moved in beside me, ready for battle.

The fireplace became a dark, bottomless hole. Grey started pawing at the door and howling, letting everyone know she was *not* a dog.

That's when all hell broke loose in the house.

ELEVEN

The tall Shadow thing lunged at me, but the Undine, with its whitish wisps, and the Sylph both moved in front of me. They combined their Elements, Water and Air, to encircle the thing in what I could only describe as a water spout. Confident Robin was okay, I moved out of the way as the Gnome reared back with her axe and started swinging at the thing's legs.

The sound of someone screaming filled the house with each stroke of the Gnome's axe. The sounds didn't affect the Elements as they worked their way around the intruding shadow. The Salamander was the only Elemental not participating, and when I looked closely at its little face, I thought I saw confusion.

With an abrupt start, the little thing turned and looked toward the front door seconds before I heard a loud crash.

"Stop!" Crwys shouted as he ran into the den and held up both hands. Bright light came out of both palms and blinded everything in the room, washing out all color and then sound.

Seconds passed before I could see again, and not as clearly as I had before. When I could make out shapes, then colors and movement, hands took me by the shoulders and guided me forward where I was promptly pushed into a chair. I caught something swimming in front of my face and I could just hear the echo of someone's voice.

It grew louder, as if they were getting closer or I was, as the image of Crwys's face blurred, then sharpened and then came into painful and bright clarity. I put my hands to my face and made a sound.

"I'm sorry. I didn't mean to use so much. Sam, I need you to focus on me. Please."

I heard Grey's claws clicking on the linoleum of the kitchen and then she had her nose in my face, licking me. I put my hands out to her and held her against me. "It's okay, girl."

But I was thinking of Crwys's words. *Use so much what? Of that damn power of yours?* I didn't say anything but I was pretty sure—no I was damn sure—he could hear me. I'd suspected for a long time Crwys could hear thoughts, or at least sense them. I felt his hand on my cheek and I tried to pull away but I was still disoriented

"What the hell did you do?"

I recognized that voice. It was Kyle.

"I stopped her from killing it," Crwys answered in a snippy tone. "I didn't realize she was so close."

"You also didn't realize her magic is actually tied into the Elementals, did you?" That was Ivan's voice and I smelled his cologne. He had moved to my side and had his hand on my shoulder.

I cleared my throat and at last the world, which seemed burnt on the edges, filled in and righted itself. "I…I think Crwys and I don't know a lot…about each other."

"That's the damn truth," Crwys said.

Blinking helped me focus until eventually I could see him much clearer. His expression wasn't one I'd seen that often on his face. Worry. His eyes were red now, without a touch of amber in them. He kept his hands on my face and never looked away. "Kyle, check Robin."

"I am. He's okay. He's unconscious and breathing."

"Robin?" I said and pulled my gaze from Crwys's. I could see the couch now. Robin was on his left side, his feet still on the floor as if he'd fallen over while sitting. I tried to get up and go to him but Ivan's hand on my shoulder and Crwys's hands on my face stopped me. I looked at Crwys. "What…why the hell did you stop me? That thing was coming after Robin."

"I'm pretty sure it was. And it was because part of it recognized him and was trying to talk to him."

Grey nestled harder against me and I scraped her neck.

"It looked more like it was going to eat him," I reached up and pulled Crwys hands away. "My Elementals wouldn't have attacked if it wasn't dangerous."

"The Elementals do what you tell them to do."

"No," I shook my head. "They won't attack innocents, even if I command it."

"She's right," Kyle said as he came up behind the still kneeling Crwys. "I've seen them downright refuse her if they don't perceive the threat as base evil or harmful."

I pointed to Robin. "He said he was talking to the ghost of Kathy and begged me to come over and see her. He said she asked for me."

"A Shadow Person actually *talked*?" Ivan said.

I looked up and back at him. "So, that was really a Shadow Person?"

"What we saw before Crwys played *lighthouse from hell* looked like one," Kyle said. "Or it looked like what we've been seeing all afternoon. That's why we wanted you to get over to that house."

Looking back at Robin, I felt a pang of guilt again. "My poor baby...he was so sure he was seeing Kathy's ghost."

"Well," Crwys said as he stood and moved away to the couch. "I'm not so sure he was wrong."

Hum... "What?"

Levi stepped in at that moment, his shades tight over his eyes and looking a bit ashy. Revenants did not like the daylight. He handed Crwys a small tablet. "Looks like you were right."

Crwys looked at the tablet and his eyes arched on his forehead. "Not me. Kyle figured this out."

My head throbbed and I had that old, familiar nausea that always happened when I tried a full on Elemental power spell and was either thwarted or interrupted. I was going to be sick, and I was going to need to sleep. There was no way of getting around either of those. I sent my apologies and thanks along my magical threads to the Elementals. And each of them answered back, if not a little pissed themselves. "Figured what out?"

Kyle held out his hand for the tablet and Crwys gave it to him.

"Yeah…but what does it mean? I don't know anything about Shadow People. And Ivan doesn't either, except for what he found on the web."

"Can somebody just talk straight to me?"

"That rules me out," Kyle quipped.

I shot him a righteous bird.

Ivan came around to my left and sat on the coffee table. He was far enough away not to be in my personal space, and close enough for my damaged vision to see him just fine. He gestured with his hands as he talked. "Remember how I showed you the instances of Shadow People I'd found on web this morning?"

I nodded.

"And then Kyle found all those messages about ghosts?"

I nodded again and made a motion that meant keep going, spit it out.

"Kyle and I went to every house that called and at every house, we saw moving shadows. And they were always like he described to you on the phone. Short and skittish. Almost shy when you approached them," he licked his lips. "When we got to the last house, and this is why we called, Crwys and Levi were already there because the home owner called them."

"They called us *and* the police?"

Crwys spoke, "Levi and I got the call because we'd been in that house two weeks ago when the owner's son was found dead at his computer."

I looked up at him. "You mean like the dead Elders?"

"The only commonality was dead at their computers. Their ages were wildly different and the cause of death was very different for this one," Crwys hooked his thumbs into the empty belt loops of his jeans. "His parents had left for a vacation in Italy."

"The kid didn't want to go to Italy?"

"No. The parents didn't want him to go. They were gone for two weeks. When they got home, they found him dead. He'd been sitting at his computer gaming."

I made a face. "People don't just die sitting at the computer while they play games."

Crwys shrugged. "We had everything in the room bagged and tagged. Coroner ruled the kid's cause of death as neglect. There were no signs of foul play on him or in the room."

"Neglect?" I shifted in my chair. "How does someone die of neglect at their computer?" I glanced at Ivan. He didn't look so good.

"Remember this morning when I asked you if Ivan knew of any others like himself?" He glanced at Ivan. "This is why I asked. I couldn't justify a kid sitting at his computer and dying. But if I thought of Matrix Guy here," he nodded at Ivan. "The way he enters the web?"

I looked at Ivan. "Is it possible?"

When he nodded I felt my stomach flip. "I've had a few experiences when I dive in and I lose track of time. I was in the web or the net, whatever you want to call it, for over twenty-four hours once. When I actually pulled out—" he blushed red and I got a pretty clear image of what he found happens to bodily functions when ignored. "I'll just say I was starving and my legs and feet went to sleep."

"Is that why you abruptly got interested in exercising and hiking?" Kyle looked at him.

Ivan nodded. "That's exactly why. That scared the crap out of me. If this guy was like me and he was diving into the Cyber World, he might have let time get away from him."

Levi spoke up, "Then that makes sense. The victim, a kid named Ronald Kennett, had pretty much starved himself to death. He started playing games and never ate, never drank and never slept. Forensics showed he'd even soiled himself before he died."

Ivan blushed again. I was right.

"Sweet Lady," I mumbled.

"It was the weirdest case we'd ever come across," Crwys said. "The parents are trying to sue somebody for their kid's death, but there's just nothing for them to grasp on to. We got a call this morning from some cyber terrorist organization requesting all information on the case be transferred to them. Including the kid's computer and his equipment."

"I'm sure Captain Prescott isn't too happy about that?"

"No she's not," Levi said. "Which is why we were over there speaking with the mother about why this cyber terrorist group would be interested in her son when these two arrived. The mom corroborated their story that she left a message with the shop saying that she'd been seeing things in the house and wanted to know if they could exorcise their home."

"Did you see another Shadow Person while you were there?"

Kyle nodded. "We did. But this one was taller and he had a hat."

"And he was pissed off," Levi said. "Thing hissed at us before it disappeared. Crwys here suddenly started calling you and when you didn't answer, we all piled in Kyle's car and Crwys led us here."

I looked at Crwys. "You knew I was in trouble."

"I knew something was wrong. But it wasn't from you," he reached out and moved his hand gently over Grey's head. "She told me."

"Grey?" I looked down at her. She looked up at me with those eyes that looked so human sometimes.

"She *is* your familiar. And," Crwys shrugged. "Your Salamander thought something was wrong."

Now that really freaked me out. "*You* can *hear* my Salamander? My Fire?"

Kyle cleared his throat. "We need to let her know the other part."

"What other part?" I was miffed. What the hell was this bastard if he could talk to Elementals?

"All the addresses you got calls from," Levi said. "With the exception of this last one and the Daemon possessed dog, were homes those kids disappeared from last month."

I gasped. "The Changelings?"

Kyle, Crwys, Levi and Ivan nodded in unison. Kyle spoke up. "I didn't put it together because I didn't have a list of all the missing children. But Levi did."

"And we've got three more messages on the store phone about the same issue," Ivan said. When everyone looked at him, he held up his phone. "I checked remotely."

Yeah, he'd checked remotely, just not with the damn phone. "This isn't a coincidence. All of the homes where the children turned on their parents are now experiencing hauntings, but they're all Shadow People."

"Looks that way," Crwys pointed to Robin. "And this is the house where his niece lived, isn't it?"

"Yeah, but that wasn't his niece that came out of the fireplace. That thing morphed into a tall, red-eyed goblin."

"Shadow People," Crwys said. "By definition, are little more than impressions. Bundles of emotions that are kinetically assembled between worlds and exist there."

"Not sure I get your explanation this time either." Ivan sat in a chair.

Levi put a hand on Crwys's shoulder. "Let me try this time, bro." His eyes shifted and became black over the whites. When he spoke his voice had a dual quality that I recognized as being the voice of the demon Ashur speaking through. "In my world, where thoughts create things in a more rapid fashion, and magic as you call it, is a much more tangible tool, there are always cast offs. Things that never grow into their full potential. The last Phantasm to rule my world liked to experiment with these things. And when she was done with them, she cast them off. With no purpose, they had no home and became little more than junk. They can move from world to world but they can never fully be a part of it," he inhaled and then sighed. "They exist between the worlds. Like things caught between two panes of glass."

"But we perceive them," Ivan said. "They're like…on a different frequency. We just aren't made to fully see them, just their impression, like Crwys said."

Ashur/Levi nodded. "That is correct. The Shadow People seen in these houses are somehow linked to the missing children."

I had a really, really bad thought at that moment. Something that terrified me more than what the Arcane Magic could do to me. "What if…what if the Shadow People aren't linked. What if these Shadow People *are* the missing children?"

TWELVE

"That's why I stopped you. We don't know what your beating up on. But as for making Shadow People from this side of things?" Crwys shook his head. "As far as I know, that can't be done."

"You just wanted to be safe. I get that." I finally pushed my chair out and stood up. I was all better now, physically. Mentally? Emotionally?

I'll get back with you on those fronts.

When he didn't answer, I put my finger in his face. "What if that *was* one of the kids? Or even worse, what if that really was Kathy and I let loose a storm of Elemental whoop-ass on her?" I hated to think or even imagine that horrific shadowy nightmare had been Kathy. Then again, it was better to find out for sure. I knew that meant contacting Tzariene.

Again.

The detective shook his head. "It can't be done."

Levi shrugged. "We don't know that. What about a Coyote Flame?"

I narrowed my eyes at Levi. "That sounds familiar. What is that?"

"It's an old doorway spell," Kyle said. "It was created as a means into the Other Worlds."

"And it's dangerous," Crwys pushed my finger away from his face. "Don't even try to make one of those. They're unreliable."

"How so?"

"Because you don't know where the other door is going to form.

They're unstable. You could create a door here with the intent of going directly into *Alfheim* and end up in an ethereal dungeon."

"I heard that world shut down," Levi said. "Someone rebooted it."

Crwys pointed at his partner. "Not now."

"I don't know about this ethereal place," Kyle said. "But Arden can tell you more about the Coyote Flame. I wasn't ever allowed to learn how they're made. That's Elder magic."

"Well, unfortunately, Arden's in jail," I rubbed at my eyes.

"No, she's not," Crwys moved around the den and looked out the window at the back yard. I knew there was a very lonely swing set out there, and a trampoline, missing the joy and laughter of children. "She made bail before we even booked her. Woman's got powerful allies. Not to mention Prescott's starting to like her."

Oh great. That was not what the city needed.

Grey pushed at my hip with her nose and I reached down to her. Weight pressed on my shoulders. I started yawning. I was going to have to sleep. And eat. My magic came directly from my own energy, and I needed to refill it. "I'm going home."

"Want us back at the shop?" Kyle asked.

"No…you go on home, Kyle. I'll take Ivan back so he can get his truck. Just come in early."

Kyle nodded.

"What about Robin?" Crwys asked. I was touched that he did.

I looked at my boyfriend, still sound asleep on the couch. He looked terrible. Even more so now. "I don't know. Is there a way to ward against these Shadow People?"

"I can do what I did for the other houses we visited," Kyle said. "I have my kit in the car. The detectives can help me if they want and then I can take them back to get their car."

"I'd appreciate it. You two okay with this?"

The detectives nodded. I gave Robin a kiss on his cheek. We were growing so far apart, he and I. With Rose's death, and Kathy's disappearance…he was falling apart.

Ivan and I didn't talk on the way back. Ivan didn't bat an eye when I turned away from the shop and pulled up next to Ina's house. We went inside and things were just as I left them. I asked him to search the house for the book, just in case the Shadow Person hadn't been able to take it and had hidden it instead.

"It's not here." Ivan and I were in the back yard, looking at the Circle. "But I can see Arcane all over that Circle. What the hell happened out there?"

"Something terrible." I looked up at the sky for a few seconds. The sun was setting, leaving behind a wash of pinks and soft oranges. "You know who Ronald Kennett is."

Ivan's head snapped around as he turned around to face me. "How did you know?"

"Because you're a lousy poker player. And you've been very picky about how much time you spend diving into the web. Almost like you were afraid something like that would happen to you because you knew it had already happened to someone else."

He narrowed his eyes at me. "This is why we came here."

"Wards are still up. There aren't any devices here that can spy on us. No one knows we're here. This is where we can tell each other secrets."

"I know yours. Now you want to know mine?"

"One of them," I leaned my head to my shoulder. "What happened?"

Ivan shoved his hands into his pockets. "I was online about a month ago—this was before any of this Arcane stuff happened. I came across an article telling how a local women's shelter had been hacked, and the worker's private information was leaked out. Two of the workers were killed a day after that information got out and I found a direct link between the hack and the deaths."

"This kid did it? He hacked and killed the two women?"

"No. His girlfriend was in one of the shelters but he didn't know which one. So he started hacking them all to find her, and when he did, he leaked the information out. This forced her to leave the shelter when the two women were attacked in their homes and killed," Ivan looked upset. "I knew this bastard was responsible for the leak, even though some hacking group calling themselves Soul Machine took credit. So I looked for him, followed the path of his hack back to his computer."

I took a step toward Ivan; terrified he was going to tell me he had something to do with this kid's murder. "What did you do?"

"I dumped his hard drive. Copied it all to another server and threatened if he ever did anything like that again I'd send evidence to the FBI of what happened. I told him to leave his ex and everyone else alone. And don't look at me like that. What I do isn't traceable because there's no IP. I don't log in through anyone's account. I just access it. So he couldn't trace me if he wanted to."

"But you traced him."

"Because he didn't know what he was doing. He was only half educated in what he was. I could sense his Cyber signature but he still worked on the assumption he had to log in to hardware, and he didn't have to."

"Could he trace where you put the information?"

"He could trace the actual information. But I don't think he ever did. When I didn't hear anything else from him and his ex didn't either, I went back to his computer." He looked down and didn't say anything else.

"You found him dead."

"Yeah…it was the scariest thing I'd ever done. I mean, I could use his webcam and see he was dead. And he'd been dead a few days. So I scrubbed everything and backed out."

"But you didn't tell the police."

"Tell them what? Hey, I can put my mind into the web and take a look into people's computers and I saw this dead guy?" he made a face. "I checked in with his parent's itinerary and knew they'd be home with within twenty-four hours of my discovery."

"What you saw…that scared you, didn't it? That he'd gotten so involved that he died."

"Yes."

"And you guys saw Shadow People in his house?"

"That's what I don't understand. These things aren't ghosts, not like we define them. If they're showing up at the houses children were taken from by Dionysus to make the Changelings, why there? There wasn't a child missing from that house."

That *was* odd. No wait...*everything* in this was odd. All kinds of pieces and nothing fitting together.

"I hope your theory isn't right," Ivan said. "About the Shadow People being the children. Did you see what your Elementals were doing to that thing?"

I winced. Yeah I had. I remembered the little Gnome chopping the Shadow Person down to size. I also remembered the screams of pain.

He put his arm over my shoulder. "Things are getting bad, Sam."

"Yeah, they are." I wrapped my arm around his back. We both faced the Circle. "There's no way you can download that book again from memory?"

"No. I tossed every byte of that infernal thing the first chance I got. I don't have any of it stored in memory. Sorry, Sam."

"Oh. Well. I just don't know why a Shadow Person would take the book. Or how. I'd made it a physical book at that point."

"Oh it was physical, but probably not stable," Ivan offered. "I made it with an expander in mind, so it would convert back to the necklace. Any great amount of pressure on it would make it pop back into its smaller shape."

"And...it would have to digitize to do that?"

"Yeah," he pulled away and looked down at me. "What?"

I pulled my phone from my back pocket and did a quick inventory of where my guns were. In my car. Right. And Grey...I felt her still roaming the house. I held the phone out to him. "Look for Arcane."

"Oh I can see it. It's in the circuitry of your phone. But it's not real..." he pursed his lips. "It's like trace Arcane."

"Say that again?"

"I mean it's like what got left behind for me when I uploaded and downloaded that book. Like ghost images of what had been there. I suggest you find a way to dump your phone to get that out of there."

"So, something Arcane was in my phone, or had to be, to leave these elements?"

He nodded vigorously. "Yeah."

"So I brought whatever it was from the shop, into Ina's house, and there it came out of my phone and grabbed the book."

Ivan didn't answer at first. Grey came out of the house and started sniffing around the grass nearby. Poor thing. Probably had to go real bad. "How did it get back out of the house?"

"Huh?"

"If you brought it in through your phone, did you take it back out through your phone?"

I stared up at him. "I don't think so. I used my phone right after it to talk to Kyle."

He snapped his fingers. "That's how it got out. It went through the connection to Kyle's phone," and then his expression changed. "Oh shit…it's in Kyle's phone!"

THIRTEEN

"But how can something that's allegedly spiritual even attach itself to a phone?"

Ivan closed his eyes. "Who said these things were spiritual?" He held out his hands, palms up and I watched as he connected to the web. I didn't know how he did it, and I wasn't going to try and suss out the logistics. It was just something I'd seen and grown to accept.

The only thing I knew for certain was the magical community, as it stood now, did not need to know that Witches like Ivan existed. It would be the same if the government ever found out about us.

I could just see the threads of wireless magic surrounding him, spinning around his fingers as he manipulated local Internet connections, security cameras and service providers. I assumed he was looking for Kyle's phone.

When Ivan opened his eyes they were green and glowing. He moved his hands and ghostly images appeared in front of him. He swiped at them like anyone would swipe at a tablet screen or smart phone, pinching things to make them smaller or using gestures to make them grow.

I saw strands of colors as he plucked through them and then centered on one strand that glittered a bright and brilliant red.

"I got him. He's on the phone with…" Ivan narrowed his eyes. "I don't know this guy. Might be somebody new he met."

"Is he at home?"

"No. He's on the road, and he's not near his house. I know the communication between the phones is red because of the Shadow entity—and it looks like the thing's trying to move from Kyle's phone to this other person's phone."

Oh shit. "Can you stop it?"

"I can cut the connection. But Kyle's just going to call him back or vice versa."

"Do it anyway. Can you shut his phone down?"

Ivan moved the strand of glittering red to the right and then widened it. "Yes. He's got that app on it to find his phone. I can shut it down, but then we won't be able to communicate with him either."

"Find out where he is first." I slapped a hand to my mouth as I fought back a yawn. I'd noticed the overwhelming fatigue settling on my shoulders since leaving Rose's house and now it was even heavier.

"I'll zero in on him with traffic cameras."

I tried to move all those pieces together in my head as I waited on Ivan to locate Kyle. The Clerics had given me twenty-four hours. That was at nine this morning. It was already closing in on six in the evening and the sun was setting. I had fourteen hours or so to find the Hammer or they were going to request a warlock. Truth was, that was taking the request to Parliament. Who knew how much longer it would take Parliament make a decision? The Magical Parliament wasn't exactly a speedy bunch. Part of me figured if I didn't find them what they needed or invent something to placate them by exactly nine in the morning, there was still time.

"Got him," Ivan said as he moved blurry images across his virtual screen and read out an address.

"That's near Arden's house."

"He might be going to see his aunt."

"And the phone wouldn't work in her house to begin with. Let's meet him over there and get that phone."

Ivan blinked a few times as the images vanished and his eyes became their beautiful light brown. "And then what?"

"You're going to force that son of a bitch out of that damn phone and I'm going to get that book back."

Thinking it in my head, it sounded really cool. Saying it out loud made me sound like a dumbass.

We grabbed Grey and got back in my Jeep and headed to Arden's.

She lived in the Garden District, not far from Anne Rice's former home. Arden lived on a corner lot in a mansion to rival any of the others on her street. The house was lit up against the night for a party when we arrived; cars parked up and down the street. I used my "park fu" and found a spot down the street from Kyle's car. I jumped out and looked inside, hoping maybe he just left the phone in the car.

No such luck. There wasn't an Arcane thing in it.

"You really want me to go in there?" Ivan looked worried as he stepped out of the Jeep. He knew how much I didn't want Arden to know what he was. He was afraid of the woman because she'd inadvertently put him in a coma when they first met. Long story.

"Yeah. I need you with me. Just don't connect with anything in the house. Can you do that?"

He nodded, but he still looked worried.

I made sure I had my guns and Grey followed at my heels as we headed to the house. The iron front gate was open and we walked in.

The place was packed—literally—with people. Everyone was dressed in nice clothing, which made our casual apparel stick out. Grey hung outside and settled in the bushes. I had the clear impression she did not want to go inside.

"Sam!"

I heard Kyle's voice as we slowly made our way through the crowd. I spotted him, waved, and the three of us met in a corner near the staircase where there were no people and no furniture. I gaped at Kyle. He was actually dressed up in a nice suit. "What's going on?"

"Fundraiser," he said as he gestured around. "I promised my aunt I'd show up and I forgot till I left Rose's house and found messages from my aunt on my phone. Crwys and Levi took a taxi back to the Kennett house."

"You keep a suit in your car?"

"Damn straight I do. Never know when you might need one," Kyle smirked. "I also keep a whole change of clothing in my trunk, along with an emergency toiletry kit."

I returned his smirk. "Nice. So, what's the fundraiser for?"

"Avondale Women's Shelter. Arden's a big supporter when it comes to domestic violence cases. Avondale is one of her most successful shelters. They were hacked about a month ago and two of their workers were killed. So this party is to raise money for their families and prove to the community that Avondale Shelters shouldn't be closed."

Women's shelter. Ivan's story about the hacker came back to me. Ivan looked like he was going to be sick. I grabbed the collar of his hoodie and brought him down to my level. "Please tell me Avondale wasn't the shelter that kid hit?"

He just stared at me.

"Shit…"

"It's worse than that," Ivan looked around before he leaned in close and spoke in my ear. "Remember how I said I hid the proof that would incarcerate him?"

Oh no.

"What are you two whispering about?" Kyle leaned in. It was hard to hear with all the people milling about and talking.

I grabbed them both by the upper arms and led them through the red room in the back, the one I always thought looked like a bordello and outside to the pool. Since it was December and cold, no one was out and the pool was covered. Which seemed odd to me since the pool was enclosed in mesh.

I faced both of them. I had Ivan update Kyle on the shelter and what he'd done to Ronald Kennett. I followed the story all the way to hearing the name of Avondale. "So now answer my question, Ivan."

The two of them looked at each other. When Kyle put his hand to his forehead, I knew it as going to be bad news. Ivan said, "Kyle asked me to hack his aunt's servers once—back when I first started working at the store. I, uh…I did it because it was easy and apparently they haven't changed their security in six months. So I found a nice, empty patch of drive real estate on one of them, upgraded the encryption and security for that particular server and…just left it there."

"Christ, Ivan," Kyle said. "You left damning evidence about this hacker and Soul Machine on one of my aunt's servers?"

"Who would ever think to look there?" Ivan shrugged. "Come on, give me a break. Think about it."

"Ivan," I said when it became clear he didn't see the correlation. "If you could find that tiny bit of real estate, who's to say somebody else couldn't? You said it yourself that it was possible he traced the information. And if he traced it there, it is conceivable he believed that someone in Arden's company, or companies, was the one that hacked him."

"Which means you set her up," Kyle ran his fingers through his thick, dark hair. "Oh damn, Sam. Do you think that's who's framing Arden for those murders?"

I held up a hand. My own brain was spinning faster than it should and I wanted to go off in search of coffee. Black. Strong. Fatigue pressed down heavy on my shoulders. "Who's framing Arden? Ronald Kennett? How? He's dead."

"Then what about killing those Elders, that is, if this guy was a Witch like Ivan."

"No…look at the timeline." Eh gads for a whiteboard! "Ivan said he hacked this guy two weeks ago. Threatened him. That puts it in the middle of the two weeks his parents were gone."

"Which means he was dead when the Elders were killed," said a new, distinctly feminine and familiar voice.

Everyone turned to see Emily Pearson step outside to the pool. She wore a little black dress that actually flattered her full size. She carried a clutch and walked expertly in high, satin black heels. She smiled as she approached and held her hand out to Ivan. "I'm Emily. I think you know what I am thanks to Samantha, but we haven't been formerly introduced."

My heart raced when Ivan shook her hand. "I'm Ivan Westerfield."

"Yes. The third and less Gifted of Sam's little band of Merry Men. She's a lot like her mother. Tends to attract the strays. So, tell me more about how you hacked this hacker? I take it this is what you do in the mundane world?"

Ivan glanced at me. I gave him a slight nod. Apparently, Emily hadn't been tipped that the hacking was a magical hacking.

I was surprised to see Grey step outside and come padding up beside me. In fact, she sat in front of me, facing Emily, putting herself between us. It would have been interesting to see the faces of the guests inside when a dog the size of a wolf came trotting through as if she knew her business.

"Yes, ma'am. I'm a computer systems analyst. Or I was."

"Before your Gift came to you?"

I must say I was impressed to see Ivan work with it. "That's exactly it! How did you know?" He feigned surprise well.

"Because it happens to all of us. And I'm sure working with computers and then having a Gift—those things didn't work, did they?"

"No, ma'am. All the magnetic fields kept buggering up."

"Emily. Please call me Emily."

"Emily."

Kyle, Grey and I did the ping-pong conversation follow, going from Ivan on the left and Emily on the right. He'd played her. Oh Sweet Lord he'd played her and he was good at it!

Something red glittered around Kyle's left suit jacket pocket. I smelled the Arcane as well as saw it. Without a signal to latch on to, the son of a bitch was trying to peak out and see where he could go. I glanced at Emily who appeared to be enthralled in conversation with Ivan. And who wouldn't be? The guy was cute as hell.

Grey nudged my hand and I petted her head. "Yeah," I said in a low voice. "I see it."

My hope was it would just stay where it was and choose a more opportune time to step out of the phone—one that didn't involve manifesting in front of a Cleric.

That just wasn't going to happen, the thing literally spilled out of Kyle's pocket and puddled on the floor. Just a flat, gooey looking mass of jellied red glitter. And if I looked hard enough, I could just see the Hammer in its flash drive form in the very center of it. Just an outline in darker red.

Three seconds after wondering if anyone else could see it; Ivan did a classic double take at Kyle. Emily looked to see what had Ivan's attention. She did a double take too.

Kyle looked at the two of them staring at him and he put his hands to his suit jacket. "What? Did I spill crab dip on myself?"

When he looked down, he made a slightly high-pitched noise and backed away from the puddle.

Guess that answered my question, didn't it?

Two seconds later the red glittering puddle was replaced by a six-foot man made of Shadow.

FOURTEEN

Yeah it was big. And scary looking. And it had my necklace around its neck.

Thief!

"What the hell is *that*?" Emily had already dropped her drink on the tiled patio as pentagrams of white formed a barrier around her. I spotted her Gnome as she jumped out of one of the pentagrams and landed with a thud in her iron boots. The thick lass shook her axe at the Shadow Person.

I too was summoning my Elementals and felt a bit of guilt when the Sylph appeared next to me yawning. If I was tired, they were tired, as they were a direct reflection of my connection to the Elements. I hadn't slept yet and we were all thinking it felt like Monday.

I nodded to the Shadow Person and the Sylph gasped as large yellow pentagrams formed all the way around the swimming pool area.

The Shadow figure darted toward the doors leading back inside. I wasn't sure if I was really juiced or if it was running really slow because…it was running really slow. Instead of a speedy sprint to the doors it was in a leisurely jog. That slow speed also gave my brain enough time to process a few ideas.

This thing had been hiding inside of electronic devices—who knew they could do that? That meant there was a possibility they were as defenseless against certain attacks as say a phone or a computer. The worst thing I could think of was a magnetic pulse. But shorting out the entirety of the Garden District wasn't on my agenda tonight.

So, I combined two of the Elements to create a concentrated static charge—we call that lightning—and sent it at the thing's back.

The Shadow seemed to short out. It blinked between being visible and not. And it slowed its advance at the doors. But that was because my Sylph's pentagrams were creating a barrier. He was siphoning off electricity from Arden's house and electrifying the fence, so to speak.

I came around one side and Ivan bolted around the other, each of us without defenses ready. Ivan got to it first and released an eerie green bolt of what looked like ones and zeros that twisted and wrapped around its body. The Shadow figure did more of that blinking off and on thing as it writhed under Ivan's assault.

Glancing at Emily, I noticed her watching Ivan a little too intensely and decided his power didn't need to be common knowledge. Not yet. So I conjured up my exorcism spell and hit it with that.

The impact broke Ivan's bolt as white and green ones and zeros danced and bounced all over the tiles. He was shoved back against the door the Shadow figure had tried to escape through. That impact brought with it a gathering of watching eyes from inside.

Shit. Most of these people were Cowens and did not need to see this. I looked up at one of the lights illuminating the pool and sent the Sylph to short-circuit it. Once it started spewing sparks, the Gnome ran over and chopped at the pole holding it.

I guided the ensuing energy at the Shadow figure, juicing it a bit more than before until it literally erupted in a sparkling display of red and dark glitter. When it was gone, I saw my necklace fall on the tiled floor. Ivan got to his feet and ran to me, bending just enough to grab the necklace, and made it look like he was getting Emily and me out of the way of the sparking light.

The pentagrams faded away as they were dismissed and those of us out at the pool came into the room.

"Thanks Ivan," I said, just loud enough for others to hear.

"Yes, young man, that was a brave thing you did." Another man said and shook Ivan's hand.

"That was just awful. Emily, are you okay?" One of the older ladies in a nice silver dress approached Emily.

I made sure to lock eyes with Emily and she gave me an almost imperceptible nod. "Oh yes, Victoria. I'm fine."

"Excuse me, hello, my party, out of my way *shugars*," Arden Vervain's voice rose above the den of talking guests as she emerged from the crowed. Arden was dressed in a lovely, deep purple gown, coiffed to the nines and not looking anything like someone who'd spent time in jail that morning.

Me?

I looked like wilted lettuce.

When she spotted us she smiled. "Sam, Ivan….I had no idea you were here. And you brought your…dog."

Grey came up beside me and several guests reached out to stroke her flank. "Yes, we came here to see you. I'm sorry to crash your party. Kyle didn't mention you were having a fundraiser tonight."

"He didn't?" she gave him a sideways look. "Interesting." Then she moved to the door leading out to the darkened patio. "I see one of my lights went out."

"Yes, Miss Vervain," a guest said. "And if it wasn't for this striking young man here, Emily and these other people could have been electrocuted!"

Heads nodded. I tried not to make a wise-ass remark.

"Oh, it was nothing," Ivan suddenly spoke up. "Just something I learned after my mom moved us to a shelter."

Okay…I called shenanigans. But he now had every eye in the house on him.

"You were in a shelter, dear?" said the woman who asked Emily if she were okay. Victoria.

Ivan nodded to her. "My mom was brought over from Japan as a mail order bride. My father was cruel to her after I was born, and if it hadn't been for places like the Avondale Shelter, we might not have survived."

I slipped back as guests surged closer to Ivan. Kyle was in the background as well, watching with an amused smirk on his face. Grey made her way out of the crowd and sat beside me. "He really knows when to put on the charm."

Kyle snorted. "You just now noticed?"

Arden stepped up and started talking to her guests as they whipped out their credit cards and checkbooks. Her little helpers, most of them members of her coven, walked around with wireless transaction machines and lockable pouches for cash.

"You do realize," Kyle said in a low voice. "Ivan's going to have my aunt eating out of his hands."

"I think that's what he intended," I looked up at him. "You okay?"

"Sure. Why wouldn't I be?"

"Well, we haven't really talked—"

"Sam, don't bring up Crwys now. Please. It's your shop, your business. If you want him to be a part of it, then fine."

"That wasn't it. I didn't want him to do it—" I held out my hands. "He just…did it. Came in and announced it to me."

When Kyle didn't answer I narrowed my eyes at him. "You don't care."

"Not really."

"What the hell is wrong with you?"

"With me? What the hell's wrong with you?"

"What?" I took a step back and Grey whined. "I'm not the one who doesn't come to work on a regular basis, and I'm not the one that disappeared for those hours two weeks ago—"

"Oh, you are *not* going to bring that up again," he turned a very unpleasant face down at me. "I had things to do, Sam. I have a life. And I keep some of my life private. I don't live it out in the open like you do for everyone to see."

His words hurt. A lot. And I didn't want to admit that to him or to myself. Instead, I kept my hand on Grey's neck and she bumped up against my leg. "You didn't tell us about this fundraiser because you didn't want us here."

"Got it in one."

"Why not?"

He held out his hands. "Hello? Look around?"

"What I'm seeing is your aunt making a lot of money for a

good cause and she's doing it because we're here. Now get the hell over yourself."

"Sure. Fine. Here comes your golden boy."

I didn't have time to ask him what he meant by that as Arden and Ivan approached us. Ivan stood by me as Arden handed a few of the money pouches to Kyle. "You got the Hammer?"

"I've already uploaded it."

I stared at his face. "You okay? Last time it looked like it made you sick."

"I wasn't used to doing it then. I've been practicing. I mean, yeah I've got a headache and I'm going to need to get rid of it as soon as I can, but I'll be all right. You want me to make a copy of it before we leave?"

"No. Wait till we get back to the shop."

There was a pause. "Sam?"

"Yes?"

"You know that didn't kill it."

"Yeah. I figured. Nothing's that easy."

"I think to actually destroy it, you're going to have to find where it's housing its base memory."

I blinked. Frowned. "Say that again?"

"I know who it is, now. When I touched it with my...whatever that was I did...I recognized its signature."

"Signature?"

"It's like a footprint. You leave it where you go. Same kind of residual energy you leave behind when you enter and leave a room, or when you cast a spell. That Shadow Person was once alive and it was just like me."

I stared at him. "You mean..."

"It's Ronald Kennett, Sam. That thing that spooked you, took the Hammer, and just tried to escape is whatever was in his computer when his body died."

"You mean...our theories were right?"

"Yeah. And what's worse?"

"There's worse?"

Ivan nodded. "He knows who I am now."

"Sam!" Arden finished with Kyle and came up to us as she put her hand on my arm. "We need to talk."

"If it's about hiring Ivan out, I'm afraid the answer is no."

She laughed as she guided us away from the dispersing guests and into her private parlor behind the grand staircase. The bordello room. Once inside, she closed the door and looked at both of us. Her smile was slow and sweet. "Inamorata has it, doesn't she?"

I wasn't sure what to think about this turn of conversation. "Has what?"

"The Hammer. I know for a fact she wanted it as much as I did."

"Uh...no. I don't think my aunt has the Hammer."

"I bet she does. And that's why she ran away. You do know she's gone, right?"

"I noticed the house was empty. She hasn't been seen since Samhain."

"The Clerics questioned me about that too." Arden moved to her wicker fan-back chair. She pointed to Ivan. "Care to tell me more about this one's very interesting Gift?"

Ivan and I glanced at one another. I shook my head. "He's Dianic."

"What I saw attack that Shadow wasn't Dianic, Samantha. In fact, it wasn't anything I've seen before. Spill it."

I stepped toward her. "You saw the Shadow?"

"When people enter rooms in my house I know it. I was watching from the room above. I saw everything. I also saw him pick something up. Something that Shadow dropped," she held out her hand. "Let me see it."

Ivan frowned at her. "I picked up this," and he pulled a USB drive out of his pocket. It wasn't the one he'd turned into the Hammer, but one I'd seen him use before. He handed it to her.

She examined it, held it out and then tossed it back to him. "One mystery solved. What Dianic Gift does he have?"

I shook my head. "Tell me what you know about the Coyote Flame."

The look on Arden's face told me that question had come at her from left field. "Why in the hell do you want to know about that?"

"It's important."

"Then you'll tell me what his power is?"

"Is it really that important?"

"Yes."

"You want me to help you clear your name and so you don't do jail time?"

Her eyes narrowed. "Yes."

"Then you don't need to know," I took a closer step. "What is a Coyote Flame? I heard it was a door into the Other Worlds."

Arden made a nasty noise. "It's a piece of Ceremonial rubbish is what it is. Damn Quinn."

"Quinn?" I didn't know if that was a name or a term.

"Quinn Ragland. Noted Magician around the turn of the century. Discovered the Other Worlds. No one knows how he did it, but he was obsessed with finding a door into what he called Other dimensions. And when he couldn't find one, he made one. Over one thousand homeless and ill innocents lost their lives with his experiment. He did it. He made a door that would take anyone from this world into another world," she held up her finger. "But, the catch was the other side wasn't stable. Eight out of ten times the door shunted its poor victims into a solid object or into that limbo between worlds."

"That's it," I pointed at her. "That's what I'm worried about. What happens to the ones caught between worlds?"

Arden looked confused. "You should know this. You just fought one."

The Shadow People.

Arden continued. "The door's magic wasn't new when Quinn found it. It was actually based off some spell he found in a book that was passed down from his grandmother and grandfather. But then it was called the Devil's Hole."

Ivan crossed his arms over his chest. "That sounds awful."

"It was supposed to. Apparently it was something the church used to get rid of sinners. Evil monsters. I'm pretty sure a few Revenants were thrown into these things over the past few centuries."

"Can…can you get out of it?"

"Only if the door's opened the same way," Arden shrugged. "But most of the time it's a one way trip." Now she leaned her head to her shoulder. "Why are you asking? Did someone make one?"

"I don't know. I'm terrified they did," I cleared my throat. "The missing children."

I counted one beat before Arden realized what I was getting at. What I was worried about. She instantly stood and came to me. "You're not serious."

"Where else are they?" I searched her face. Arden was beautiful. Ageless. I often wondered if she had children of her own somewhere, or was she really as young as she looked? "They're not in this world."

"That's…that would be an abomination."

I looked past her to Ivan. "Tell her what you and Kyle saw today."

I moved around to the fire as Ivan recounted the different experiences he and Kyle had in each of the homes with the small and almost playful Shadow People. I came back to them and told her about my experience at Rose's house and how Crwys stopped me.

"This is bad," Arden said. "We have to know if they're in there."

"I thought about asking Tzariene if she knew if they were in *Alfheim*."

"No. Not Tzariene. You have to ask Brendi."

Brendi? "No. That's not gonna happen."

"You have to. You said Brendi made a deal with that Leviathan for Medbh's head, didn't you? It is possible she knows exactly what that bitch did to those children," Arden looked as stricken as I felt. "We have to ask Brendi."

"But I don't have anything else to give her, and the only reason she hasn't taken me is because she promised her dad."

"I'll ask. In fact, we'll cut the Circle here. With my people and I'll ask. I'll offer her something."

"What?"

"Doesn't matter. Let's get this done. And hope she knows—*if* they were cast into a Coyote Flame—where."

"Where is important?"

Arden reached out and touched my cheek. "Only if you want to get them out."

FIFTEEN

We made plans to meet Arden at Gypsy Gardens, her estate outside the city along Lake Pontchartrain at midnight. That gave us around three hours to get to the shop, change and get a few ritual supplies I wanted to use. It also gave Arden time to call out to her house and get them ready. She wouldn't tell me what she planned on exchanging for the information.

And that worried me.

Once in the shop, Kyle ran upstairs to my apartment and changed into jeans, shirt, sneakers and jacket. He also stored his ritual robes up there as well. I asked him to grab mine. Ivan didn't have any yet, since up until that point we really hadn't had any reason to cut a Circle.

I was in the back office grabbing my ritual bag when I heard Ivan yell out. It wasn't a call for me—but more like a "Hey somebody!"

I dropped what I was holding, pulled my guns out my bag and headed back to the front as Kyle came thundering down the steps. I burst through the door with my guns up just as five men in black suits turned and pointed their guns at me. Ivan stood in the middle of them, handcuffed and looking terrified.

Dammit. It was like Halloween all over again. Only this time I could see the black suited ninjas. "Drop it right there because I'm calling the police!"

"Please, go right ahead Miss Hawthorne," the tallest of them said. He was the only one without a gun. And upon further examination of their guns—they had really *big* guns. He reached into his pocket and pulled out a black wallet. "Please, allow me to introduce myself."

I kept both of my guns focused on him as he stepped forward and held the wallet open. "My name is Special Agent Pierce Goddard. My team and I are here to take Mr. Westerfield in for questioning."

I looked at the badge and my *dex* launched. It wasn't just good for identifying species. It could see lies as well. And from what it could tell of the ID, this was legit. But that didn't mean I was putting my weapons down. It'd been that kind of day. "Questioning for what?"

"Sam, you can put your guns down," Kyle said to my left.

"Not until they do and they take the cuffs off Ivan."

Goddard nodded to his right, then his left, and the men all lowered their weapons. "I'm afraid the cuffs have to stay. Procedure."

"Is he under arrest?"

"No. Not yet. But he is wanted for questioning in conjunction with the actions of a black hat group calling themselves Soul Machine."

"Ivan doesn't have anything to do with them."

"I'm afraid we've been given information that says otherwise. And given Mr. Westerfield's past history with computers and hacking, we think he'd benefit from our protection."

Protection? "You're not taking him."

Goddard reached into his jacket pocket again and retrieved a folded piece of paper. He handed it to Kyle who skimmed it. "What the hell? You're shutting us down?"

"Just your Internet. While we conduct our investigation to see if Mr. Westerfield has information that pertains to Soul Machine and the deaths of three elderly men."

"What does that mean, shut down our Internet? For how long? I have to make orders. I have an online presence." I honestly didn't know if I did or didn't. Ivan took care of all that stuff. I wouldn't call myself a Luddite, but I was in the ball park.

But let's face it. Magic and technology? Not exactly the best match.

One of the guys in suits stepped forward and offered me his hand. He literally stood in front of my guns, blocking my view of Goddard and Ivan and stuck his hand out. "Ma'am. My name's Jack Roberts. I'll be handling the shut down. And I promise, I won't damage any of your equipment."

Equipment? We had equipment?

The other men in black started moving, escorting Ivan out the front door.

"Get out of my way, Jack."

"Ma'am—"

I fired one of the guns just past his left ear. He moved.

The bullet struck the wall over the agents' heads and they all aimed their guns at me again.

"Sam…" Kyle sounded a bit on edge. "You're tired. And stressed out. They'll talk to Ivan and find out he has nothing to do with this so-called group and they'll release him."

"Miss Hawthorne," Agent Goddard said. "I was told to treat you with kid-gloves. But if you don't lower your weapons I will shoot you myself."

"Sam," Ivan said from where he was held by the door. "Just do as he says. And remember what I said at Arden's?"

What he said at Arden's? I flipped through what I could remember and then…*oh shit.*

Kyle stepped next to me and pushed my left arm down. I lowered both arms and watched as they took Ivan away and filed out of my shop. All of them except Jack Roberts.

"Get out."

"Ma'am, I'm supposed to take your router. I have a warrant."

I narrowed my eyes at him. "Then take it and get the fuck out of my shop before I blow your ass off." I turned and headed into the back room.

I was shaking when I set both guns on the table. I was so tired. And the night wasn't over. No, but it sure as hell just got a lot more complicated. I was depending on Ivan to download that book so—

DAMMIT!

He still had the Hammer…and now some weird ass spooks had him.

Unless they weren't real spooks.

Oh shit. What if this was like last time, and Dionysus was behind it again? He'd set up a new group with men this time and now they had Ivan. Again!

My phone rang and I irritably pulled it out of my pocket. When I saw Pauline's number I refused the call and held tight to the phone.

Who the hell could I ask? I needed to make sure they were legit. I wasn't going to be able to function if I didn't know for a fact those were real agents. Checking up front, I listened and heard Kyle talking with Jack.

I dialed the only number I knew.

"Wow…this is a rare event."

"Shut up, Crwys. I need you to tell me that the agents that just came and picked Ivan up are legit."

"Wait…what? Slow down. Agents just picked Ivan up? For what?"

I blabbed it all. Well not *all*. Most of it. I started where Ivan found out about the leak at the women's shelter and ended at the fundraiser, wrangling pretty well around the Hammer.

He whistled. I had learned this to be a good thing with him. It meant he'd been listening and he was interested. "Ivan's betting this Ronald Kennett sent the feds some bullshit about him being involved."

"I also suspect Kennett's the one that set Arden up with the three dead Elders."

"How so?"

"Because Ivan hid the information he had on Kennett on one of Arden's company's servers."

"Is it still there?"

"I have no idea."

"I'm gonna need that." Crwys said something to somebody and then, "Give me the agent's name."

"Pierce Goddard."

He paused. "That's the same agent that came asking us about Soul Machine and Ronald Kennett. The one I told you about? Runs a cyber terrorist task force across Mississippi and Louisiana. Kennett knew right where to send the stuff. Look, I'll see what I can do about helping Ivan. You go through with the ritual at Arden's. If I get good news, I'll either bring it to you or call you."

I felt a small bit of relief. Small. Mostly I felt guilt because I still hadn't told him everything. "I'll try."

"Sam...when was the last time you slept?"

"This morning." I hung up and shoved the phone back in my pocket. I saw the red three on the phone icon and knew Pauline had left messages. But I couldn't head out to Picayune just yet.

I had a small bathroom built just off of my office. It wasn't much, just a toilet and a sink, but one thing it was, was private. I locked myself in there for a few minutes to mediate. I know, meditating in the bathroom sounds weird. But don't knock it. Best place to sit and regroup.

Until someone knocks on the door.

Knock, knock, knock. "Sam?"

I hung my head. "Is it time to leave?"

"Yeah...no...I don't know. But I need you to come out here. We have a problem."

Again?

I was pretty sure this problem had something to do with Jack Roberts, so I took my time and splashed water on my face, raked my fingers through my unruly mass of hair, took two more deep breaths and stepped out. Luckily, neither of them was in my office. I grabbed my bag and looked for them. They were in the break room.

"Sam—" Kyle said as he put his hands on the table. "Jack has a slight problem."

"Really? How nice," I set the bag on the table. "We have to go."

"I am really sorry ma'am," Jack said with his hands out. "But I can't find your modem or your router."

Jack really was a nice looking guy, in a sort of geeky way. He was a nice build, a little too wiry for me. His hair was cut pretty short on the sides and back. A nice brownish color. Reminded me of chocolate pudding.

My stomach growled at the thought of pudding. I wondered if there was yogurt in the fridge. So I went to it to see. Yay! There was an Oikos! I grabbed it and looked for a spoon. "What is that?"

"The modem is the device that—"

"No. Stop," Kyle waved his hands in the air. "Both of them make Wi-Fi possible. But he can't find ours."

Omg…this yogurt was so good. I ate half of it before I asked, "Do we have either of them?"

"I thought we did. I mean, I get Wi-Fi on my phone."

"Is it *our* Wi-Fi?"

They both looked at me. I really was listening. But I'd left all of this up to Ivan, and it was obvious to me the person they had to ask was Ivan.

Kyle narrowed his eyes. "Are you saying we don't have Wi-Fi?"

"I don't pay a Wi-Fi bill. So I would suggest to you," I pointed my spoon at Jack Roberts. "That you should be asking Ivan Westerfield, the innocent man your people just dragged out of here. I don't pay a bill on a Wi-Fi. You won't find a bill for it in my name. This shop doesn't have Wi-Fi. It's a magic shop. Magic and wireless don't get along."

I turned and finished the yogurt before I tossed the empty container into the trash.

Jack looked at me, then at Kyle. "Is she serious? Magic?"

"Yep. We're a magic shop."

"Magic isn't real."

I waved at him. "Get out. Kyle, in the Jeep," I turned and looked up the stairs to my apartment. "Grey! We're going!"

Kyle had his bag packed and hoisted it over his shoulder. "You can walk out this way."

"Is the front locked up?"

"Oh, let me make sure," Kyle disappeared through the door just as Grey came down the steps.

When she saw Jack, she stopped at the bottom of the steps and growled at him. Her ears flattened and she showed some teeth.

"Grey, stop that. This is Jack the G-Man," I looked at him.

His teeth were clenched tight and he looked like he was actually going to growl back at her. I waved my hand in front of his face. "Hey, you. Get a grip."

He blinked and pointed at Grey. "That's a wolf."

"Yes."

"A *real* paladin."

I frowned at that. "A what?"

Kyle breezed back in. "Okay. All locked up. We're good."

"Fine. Show the G-Man out. We've got less than an hour to get there." I watched as Kyle escorted Jack Roberts out the back. I also watched as Jack and Grey kept looking at one another. Why had he called her a paladin? Was that a type of wolf?

I followed them out with Grey beside me. I got in Kyle's car and Grey jumped into the back. I would have liked to take my Jeep, but my top had a rip in it and given New Orleans's rain lately—I didn't want a wet butt.

Kyle came jogging back and slid into the driver's seat.

"Where's your G-Man?"

"He went around front." Kyle looked around as he backed the car out and then pulled out onto Bourbon Street. "You think he's cute?"

"Who? Jack?" I winced. "If you like the government type."

"I think he's cute."

"Is he *family*?" Translation, is he gay?

"Oh I'm sure of it," Kyle smiled at me.

I glanced at him and saw that dopey, dreamy look he always got when he fell in love. But be advised, Kyle fell in love every other Thursday. "Wipe your drool and get in the mood. We're gonna be talking to Brendi." I shivered at that.

Brendi. The Obsidian Queen of the Unseelie Court. The first Queen of the Faerie Realm.

Thinking of this made the yogurt curdle in my stomach.

SIXTEEN

I was glad Kyle drove out to Gypsy Gardens. I was still too rattled from the G-Men taking Ivan. I mean come on…whose life is like this besides mine? I didn't mean to sound like I'm whining, even though I am, but…damn. I couldn't catch a break lately.

Grey knew I was wiped both mentally and physically at this point and kept her head on my shoulder from where she sat in the back. I didn't know how I functioned without her before. She wasn't like the usual familiar, not a companion I just drew energy from for magic. She was more of a constant companion. There was something familiar about her that I could never quite put a finger on.

Arden's plantation—because let's face it, that's what it was—sat just outside of New Orleans along the border of the Bayou Sauvage National Wildlife Refuge. Though most of the land was considered a swamp, the water itself fed into Arden's Elemental Gift of Water and worked as a killer power base. The land had been in her clan for generations. I use the word clan because Arden came from a long line of gypsies that stole the land from white settlers over a century ago, gave up their wandering ways, and worked magic with the land.

The plantation sat at the end of a long drive of moss-covered trees. The scene always reminded me of the plantation setting in the movie *Interview with the Vampire*. My heart jumped into my throat as Kyle sped along that sandy drive.

I counted around sixteen cars parked in the lot in front of the house. All of them high end. BMWs, Mercedes, Lexus…and then there was Kyle's Prius. At least I knew Kyle was keeping up with the planet's care and maintenance and not the Joneses.

The moon wasn't visible; it was in its dark phase since it was full on Samhain. The winter air was crisp as I grabbed my leather jacket out of the back and put it on, then strapped holsters on my thighs and slipped my guns into them. I didn't use the custom made holsters much because they were showy, but I felt that tonight I needed as much showy as I could get.

"I don't think my aunt's going to want those in the house."

I glared at Kyle as he grabbed his own bag out of the trunk, but I didn't comment. I was a little worried what would come out. Part of my mind was thinking about Ivan, knowing he still had the Hammer uploaded inside of him, somehow. Another part was thinking about the Clerics' threat of warlocking and the fact I had less than nine hours left to find their damn book for them. Another facet of my multitasking was thinking about these children and feeling guilty—because if what I think is true and they're not in *Alfheim*, then I've left them in that limbo for over two weeks!

All my own childhood fears of trust and dependence on adults came back to me. I relived my own feelings of anger and doubt when my mom vanished. And I hated that temporary feeling of betrayal I'd had, until the police said she'd died in the line of duty. I didn't want these children thinking any of these things about me.

No…not all of them.

Just Kathy. I knew Kathy. I knew what potential she had, because she was a God Mother's child.

Once I had my bag over my shoulder and he'd locked the trunk back, we started toward the well-lit house. Several women in long black robes greeted us. Kyle and I were ushered into a grand, if not overstated, bathroom on the lower floor, while Grey was asked to remain on the porch.

Once the door was closed, I dropped my bag and looked around. The ceiling had to be close to fourteen feet high. The walls were white with gold patterns raised on them. The carpet was a deep red and soft beneath my boots. Once I got past the notion of carpet in a bathroom,

I noticed there were two claw foot tubs, each with matching side tables laden with all the necessary accoutrements of a ritual bath.

The whole thing looked like something out of a French movie about King Louis.

Kyle set his bag on a chaise near the left tub. "There's a partition we can pull out if you want privacy."

"Arden seriously goes all out."

"She's into ritual and behaviors," Kyle shrugged. "You know the reasons."

"Yeah it's a gestalt, all minds thinking alike. I just…I don't take the ritual bath that often."

Kyle smirked at me. "Do you remember how?"

I shot him a bird and walked to the tub on the right. There was no need for a partition. This wasn't a sexual thing and besides, it was Kyle. Steam rose from the water already in the tub and I started taking my clothing off. "She's even got the script on the table. Laminated."

"Yep."

We took our ritual baths in relative silence. I hadn't been kidding when I said I didn't normally take them. I felt as if I never had time, and before I actually stepped into the water, I was thinking that same thing in an irritated, rushed way.

But once the bath began and I blessed the water with the four Elements, sat down and began the visualizations, something happened that hadn't happened for a long time.

I *relaxed*.

The stress I'd been carrying *in* my shoulders, along my neck and in my back released as it all flowed into the water. I closed my eyes and breathed. Really…breathed in the Air. Felt the water's Fire in the heat. Let the Water rinse away the bad. And I mentally touched the Earth I realized was set beneath the tub in a long rectangular box.

After the bath, I felt rejuvenated and dressed in my ritual robe. This was something I hadn't worn since I moved out of Ina's house and I was afraid it wasn't going to fit me.

And I was right. But it wasn't too tight. It was a bit loose. Ritual robes by themselves weren't always flattering. They had a purpose for those who didn't go sky clad (nude) so as not to close off the energy needed to flow to and from the Witch.

Ina made mine, and she made it a little more form fitting than most. It was sewn in a Greek style of toga, with black natural material cinched at my shoulders and then cut in at my waist. The rest of the robe fell down around my hips and legs, and just brushed the carpet at my feet.

I reached into my bag and pulled out my mother's athame, the one I'd taken from Ina's house. It still glittered with bright Arcane Magic and I decided this wasn't the time to use it. I shoved it back into the bag and zipped it up just as Arden came into the bathroom.

Her gown was similar to mine; only she had long sleeves that ended in tatters. Part of the design reminded me of Morticia's dress from *The Addams Family*. Her hair was pulled back at the base of her neck and she wore no make-up. She looked so much younger like this and I wondered again exactly how old she was.

She took Kyle's hands and kissed his cheeks. His robe was what I called the standard monk's robe, with a hood and long skirt. And then she looked at me and put her hands to her mouth. "I'm sorry, Samantha, but you look so much like your mother."

I took that as a compliment. "I ah…I don't have an athame."

"It's fine. You won't need it. My initiates are already cutting the Circle," she looked around. "Where's Mr. Westerfield?"

I sighed and gave her a short version of what happened at the shop, and a bit of the background of why. I left out the bits about the shelter and about where Ivan hid the information on Kennett he threatened to use. Her dark eyes nearly popped out of her head. "And you think the soul or essence of this Ronald Kennett is framing him?"

"Yeah I do. I talked to Detective Holliard. He's going to look into Ivan's problem while we solve this one. Right now, my goal is to find the kids."

"And then clear my name."

I pulled my mouth into a thin line and held my temper. Wow. That bath really did good things for my mood control. "Of course, Arden."

We were led through the house, which was just as spectacular as the bathroom with its high ceilings and antique furniture. We passed a long dining table laden with food as we made our way out the back French doors and down a path. I didn't go barefoot much anymore and it was obvious, given I found every possible sharp rock and stick with the soles of my feet.

I sensed the Circle before I saw it. It hummed and pulsed against my spine and my Spirit sang at the connection between the Earth and us. This was the God Mother's legacy. This was Diana's joy. All minds concentrating on a single thought, a single note, a single song.

As with the Circle Ina's Ghouls made that night when I spoke to Tzariene, the Priestess of the Circle, a thin blond girl with dark eyes, cut the doorway. We were challenged and then brought in to stand to the north behind the Altar. Arden had already explained she thought this was the best place for me, since the Obsidian Queen was the Unseelie Court and they were more attuned to Air and Water.

The Circle's power pricked at my spine as Arden and three others stepped forward with their athames, they cut a Circle within a Circle. Light flared and after the spell was complete, I held my breath as Brendi appeared in the center.

She looked as radiant as ever, and less human as well. Her skin had taken on the paler tones of the Faerie, and her hair was now black. Slight points at the tips of her ears betrayed her acceptance of her new position. I hadn't noticed those things about her when she appeared in Couturie Forest and took Medbh in her deal with Dionysus. But she'd been wearing a helm then. All silver. All badass.

It was hard to believe this girl had once been human.

Arden curtsied before her. Brendi bowed as well. And it was Brendi that spoke first. "'Tis good to see you, Queen Arden. What, may I ask, is the reason for the summons?"

Queen Arden? I glanced at Kyle. He winked. I rolled my eyes.

"I have need of information—and I believe it is dire, my Queen. It deals with the children Dionysus stole in order to disgrace Faerie Magic and create his Changelings."

"Yes," Brendi frowned. "I have not yet forgiven him of this transgression. Yet he did offer up a payment I could not refuse."

Yeah, I bet. The bastard had tricked me into sucking Medbh's soul or essence or whatever it was into a magic necklace. Medbh's head was still in my basement. Though I couldn't figure out why Brendi would want it. It was Medbh's throne she took. Why bring the old queen back? But I didn't dare ask. Asking meant payment. I owed enough to Brendi.

"I see. May I offer a similar payment?" Arden turned and one of the girls stepped forward to be seen by Brendi in the Circle. "Branwen wishes to offer herself for the information."

What! I started forward but Kyle and two other robed members held me back. Kyle put his finger on my lips and shook his head. Why wasn't he more upset that his aunt was offering up human sacrifice?

Brendi moved with a fluid grace I hadn't noticed before. She looked at the young girl, who dropped her robe, nude beneath, and turned so the queen could see her. "Child, do you know what it means to be in my service?"

"Yes, my Queen."

I narrowed my eyes. *I* didn't really know what that meant.

Brendi smiled and looked back at Arden. "I assume your questions are many if you wish to give up the life of a human."

"They are."

"Ask them. I will decide when we are finished."

I noticed Arden's hesitation as she nodded to Branwen. The girl pulled her robe back on and returned to her place in the Circle. "I need to know where Dionysus placed the children he stole. I had believed they were with you in *Alfheim*, and were now part of your court."

"No. He did not. Such a thing would have been an honor paid to us, but he took a more foolish and selfish route," she laughed and for a second I saw the old Brendi, the human girl of sixteen. "He took the easy way out."

"He used a Coyote Flame?"

"Yes. He used it like a zipper in the fabric of space. And one by one he took the children, stole a piece of their essence to make the Changelings, and then shoved them into the Flame."

I closed my eyes. God damn that bastard. That was what I was afraid he'd done.

"Doing this, did he create what we call Shadow People?"

"He created what we know as *Dae Rauko*. The Shadow Demon," Brendi looked worried. "These *Rauko* are created from punishment, from sadness and disease. When creatures misuse the Coyote Flame and trap a being in that place of limbo, they will eventually die and become the essence of evil. Anger, frustration, feelings of abandonment, hate, all of these things fester and form to create the *Rauko*. They become *Dae*, or shadow, and they find their way into the other worlds." She took a step closer to the Circle she peered through. "These children are damned."

"Is there a way to get them out?"

"Only if you know where they were placed. Coyote Flames are not stable. You know this. You can never accurately guess where you will end up if you create one. Or choose what world. The only way to make a stable one is through human ritual sacrifice."

I didn't even want to think about what that meant. I could believe Dionysus would do this, as he would want to put all his assets in one place. But this was something so dark, so...*wrong*. My stomach roiled at the idea that this bastard had raised me.

"How do I find where Dionysus made the Flame, if he did indeed make a stable one?"

Brendi's gaze moved from Arden to me. Those around me looked at me and stepped away. No one liked being in the direct line of sight of a Faerie. "Ask Samantha. He was her guardian all along. Perhaps she can shed light on where the Leviathan would feel most comfortable."

I swallowed and ignored everyone's eyes. I was looking directly at Brendi. "I would think it would be at Ina's house."

Brendi held out her arms. "Then you have your answer." When she looked back to Arden I almost fell on my ass as my knees gave out. Kyle grabbed me and held me up.

"I thank you, Obsidian Queen," Arden stepped back.

"Not yet," Brendi held up her pale hand. "I have decided not to take this young girl, though she will receive my favor if she ever finds herself in *Alfheim*. I will instead defer my price for a later date."

Oh shit. That was so close to the same deal she'd made with me.

And I'd had to renege on it because her request was too outlandish. She'd wanted me to hand over another human being to a Succubus so he could bring that human to her.

No. Sorry. Couldn't do that.

Arden glanced back at me. "How does that work?"

"The deal is bound to you, Queen Arden. When I know what it is I want, I will contact you and tell you. You will have twenty-four hours to deliver my request, or you will forfeit yourself," she smiled and I thought for a second I saw sharp teeth. "Until later, Queen Arden."

The inner Circle darkened and then disappeared. Arden stood still for a few seconds before she nodded to the Priestess. The Circle was taken down and everyone departed to the house. Kyle and I stood where we were since Arden hadn't moved.

Eventually, she turned toward us. I saw hurt and fear in her eyes as she put a hand against my cheek. "You'd better hope she doesn't want something I can't deliver. I'll trade you before I become that bitch's dog."

I watched her walk away.

Kyle put his hand on my shoulder. "She didn't mean that."

My body shook as I put my own hand on his. "Oh yes she did."

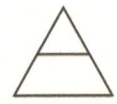

SEVENTEEN

Arden made the arrangements to move the party to Ina's house. Kyle and I changed back into our street clothing and led the caravan of three vehicles—Kyle's car, Arden's SUV and a truck—back into town and into the Garden District. It was already after three in the morning, so the streets in the district were pretty much empty. The same couldn't be said for Bourbon Street.

I didn't know how to make a Coyote Flame and said as much to Arden, but she insisted it was something she needed to do and I didn't have to learn. I wasn't blind to her real motivations. If this worked, and those children were brought back, then her involvement meant points for her run for High Witch.

I opened the house and let everyone in. Arden brought five of her finest, as she called them. And that was including Arden. Kyle and I were introduced to each of them.

I tended to connect names to attributes.

Joan was tall and thin and was the oldest of the group.

Annie had long dark hair, dark lips, dark nails and spoke in a soft voice.

Adrian wore a *Club Hell* t-shirt, the same one I slept in.

And Dayle spelled her name with a Y. Though that wasn't how I remembered her name and face. It was her ample breasts that clued me in.

The girls were each sent away with an assignment before Arden pulled Kyle and I into the herb room. She lowered her voice. "That Circle isn't fit. What happened to it?"

Shit. What was I going to say? *Oh yeah, sorry. I killed someone using Arcane Magic?*

Kyle spoke up. "Probably something Dionysus did to it before he killed that girl and disappeared."

"What girl?"

I glared at Kyle. Good going there, idiot. "Ah…it's a long story, Arden."

"And one I'm going to enjoy hearing about, especially when we sit down to talk about Mr. Westerfield."

I pointed at her. "Not if you want your name cleared."

Arden narrowed her eyes as she looked at me, then back to Kyle. "We're lucky because I don't think that's where he concentrated his Coyote Flame."

"How so?" Now I was curious how she knew that.

"Because of the way they're made, if you remember? I think the entire garden back there is what he used to tether the Flame."

When Kyle and I looked confused, she shook her head. "Take off your shoes, invoke Spirit," she looked at Kyle. "Bring lit incense with you," and then at both of us. "And walk widdershins. You'll know what I mean."

Kyle grabbed a stick of incense out of his bag before the two of us went to the sliding glass door in the dining room. We removed our shoes and I lit the incense with a pass of my hand. Kyle waved it in the air to douse the flame and once the smoke was good and thick, we stepped out onto the grass.

Walking widdershins, counter clockwise, was something I'd never done in a circle. Where clockwise, or deosil, was building or creating; widdershins was the act of tearing down. And after our first rotation around the edge of the garden, I invoked Spirit. Kyle waved his incense.

Within seconds I was overcome with weighted impressions of fear, remorse, betrayal, shock, anger, frustration, and despair… Everything toppled on me so hard and fast I crashed to the ground and was instantly surrounded by dozens more of negative emotions.

Sam!

I put my hands over my head to try and block all of them out as they wove around my own similar feelings. They fed on my fear of being in this Circle and then pulled out my own guilt over Arwen's death.

Sam! Please, baby! Dismiss Spirit.

I held onto that voice and I knew it was right. I had to dismiss the thing that fed those ghosts of past injustice away. I took in a deep breath and yelled, "So mote it be!"

The silence in my head was deafening, until I felt hands on my arms. I smelled Kyle's incense and looked up to see him looking down. Grey was right there, licking my face and pushing her nose against my cheek. I reached out and grabbed that wolf as hard as I could. I felt her lean into me and I blinked back tears.

"Sam…it's okay," Arden said somewhere behind me. "Do you understand now?"

I nodded. But I couldn't speak for fear of blubbering like an idiot.

"He killed people here. In this garden. And he did it for years," Kyle said.

And he'd done it even while I lived with Ina. Oh Goddess… how many of those guests Ina had taken in and I'd met, broken bread with and shared time with had Dionysus killed over the years? So many that vanished and Ina said they had just moved on because they were transient.

They were here…all buried beneath the grass.

"We need to start," Arden said as I sat back but still held on to Grey. "Kyle, I need you and Sam to watch, okay? Same as with the Circle at my place, just observe. Usually Coyote Flames aren't built within Circles, but I want sacred space. I want there to be no mistakes. And Sam…bring Grey with you. I don't think I truly realized what a great asset she is for you until now."

I nodded but I didn't look up. I was wiping my eyes, realizing no one else had seen my break down. Just Kyle, Arden and Grey.

And then a very warm hand touched my hand. I looked over to see the familiar masculine hand of Crwys Holliard. He took my hand in his and helped me stand. Grey wagged her tail and sat at my feet as I looked up into his amber red eyes. "What....what're you doing here?"

"Arden called me. Filled me in. I'm here in case you do get those kids out. A police presence you might say. Levi's here too, with a few more Revenants. They're patrolling the house's perimeter. Just in case something goes wrong."

"Like what?"

He brushed a tear from my cheek with his thumb. "It's a door, Sam. Doors swing both ways."

Oh. He meant in case something else comes out besides the children. I'd seen Crwys's power. I knew what he could do. I just didn't know what he was. And that was really starting to bug me.

That's when someone screamed.

Crwys was gone from my side in the blink of an eye as everyone ran back inside. The single scream became a chorus of them.

I ran behind Kyle with Grey at my heels, back in through the glass doors to the kitchen. One of the girls, Annie I think, was crying as she gripped her throat by the kitchen sink. Dayle had her arms around her, talking to her in a gentle voice. Another girl, Joan, sat on the floor, breathing into a paper bag with Adrian at her side.

"What the hell happened?" Crwys asked as Kyle, Grey and I arrived.

Arden stood in front of the door to the TV room, a spoon in her hand. It was one of the wooden kitchen spoons and not her athame. "We've got company. Apparently somebody doesn't want us to do this."

Company? In the TV room?

I ran around the other way to the door that fed from the formal living room to the TV room and stopped just inside the door. I heard Crwys's boots stop just behind me and Grey's growl as she brushed against my legs.

Standing either in the center of the room or against the back wall of the room, depending on one's perspective, were three very distinct shadowy figures. They were all human-like in form, but with no features.

I glanced at Arden on the other side of the room, blocking the door into the kitchen. "Did they try to get past you?"

"Joan and Annie were in here changing when they appeared and knocked both of them down."

"They tried to choke the women," Crwys said. It wasn't a question.

"Yes," Arden said. "So I used a basic ingredient to put up a barrier."

I looked at her feet. Salt. She'd spread it out in a line across the threshold. But they were shadows. Why not just go through the walls?

"These aren't like the ones we saw before," Kyle said. He was just behind Arden looking in. "These look like full grown people. Sam, this is like the one at Rose's house."

The Shadows reacted to him and moved toward the door. Arden held up the wooden spoon, which flashed a brilliant white. They moved away with their hands—or what looked like hands—up to protect them.

I moved further into the TV room and got the attention of all three.

"Sam..." Crwys said.

"If they attack me, burn them."

"Burn them? How am I going to burn shadows?"

Eh....good point. I thought about the one I'd fought in Rose's house and decided it might not be a bad idea to call in reinforcements. I just hoped I had enough juice. With a wave of my arms, I summoned my Elements just as I had before. All four of them appeared in their physical forms and waited for my signal to attack the Shadows.

But instead of attacking the way the Shadow had at Rose's house, all three of them moved back into a huddle in the far corner.

"They know what you're doing," Arden said.

"Oh wow...is that what an Elemental Witch can do?" one of the girls said from behind Arden. "Those little guys are so cute!"

"Yes it is," Arden said. "Now hush."

Crwys stepped into the room with me. My Salamander looked ridiculously happy to see him and actually moved over to sit on the detective's shoulder. That...was weird. "I've never seen Shadow People react intelligently."

"So you have seen them."

"Yeah. I told you, they're junk. The extra pieces of dough after you punch cookies out."

I slowly turned and *looked* at him.

He shrugged. "I bake."

"Wait," Kyle said as he disappeared and I heard him running around to the other side. He came in behind Crwys and I. "Sam, ask your Sylph and your Salamander to play a game with them."

Now Crwys and I slowly turned and looked at Kyle.

He waved his hands. "Never mind. Did Ina keep a flashlight?"

"Kitchen drawer."

"I'll get it," Dayle said. Within seconds she was at the other door and handing Kyle the flashlight.

He stepped past us to the coffee table and pointed the beam at us. When he straightened, he looked at the Shadows. "If you don't want her Elementals to tear you all a new asshole, or even an original one, listen carefully. One flash for yes. Two flashes for no. Do you understand?"

The flashlight flashed once.

Well I'll be damned.

"Well I'll be damned," Crwys put his hand to his chin.

And here we had the beauty and elegance of a Hedge Witch in action. Kyle held out his hands. "Were you human?"

One flash.

"Recently?"

One flash.

"Did you mean to hurt the girls?"

One flash.

I gave them evil looks.

"Were you trying to find a way back?"

One flash.

Kyle glanced back at me before he asked. "Were you once three Elders of New Orleans?"

There was a pause and then one flash.

I gasped. "These are the dead Elders?"

One flash.

"How," Crwys said. "How in the hell did they get like this? Wait, that's not yes or no," he licked his lips. "Did someone make you like this?"

One flash.

"Was it Dionysus?"

Two Flashes.

We glanced at each other. "Was it another Shadow Person?"

One flash.

I cleared my throat. "Was it Ronald Kennett?"

One flash and the light stayed on. Thunder vibrated the house and I felt it under my feet. Everyone made a noise of surprise as the Shadows disappeared or seemed to melt into the corner Shadow…and then that Shadow grew wide and tall until it bent against the ceiling and towered over us. Red eyes showed in the Shadow as a mouth with tiny, silver teeth opened up and laughed.

That laugh boomed over us and I looked at my Salamander. "Kick its ass."

But just before I was about to repeat the Elemental showdown, the Shadow vanished.

I dismissed the disappointed Elementals and Arden, Kyle and I did a magical sweep of the house.

"I think it's gone," Arden stood in the center of the TV room. She looked irritated.

"Did it look like the big one ate, or absorbed the little ones?" Kyle was the first one to venture what I was thinking.

"Yeah, it did," I said and put my hands on my hips. "Let's get that Coyote Flame built before it decides to come back."

Half an hour later, Kyle, Crwys, Grey and I witnessed the Coyote Flame. And that's pretty much what it was. A huge, purple flame. Arden tethered it to a spot in the north where my Gnome stood guard.

I was pretty sure no one else saw the red glitter within the Flame. I wasn't sure if the magic was Arcane, but the connection was. I stepped out in front of the Flame at Arden's gesture and called out Kathy's name. After several minutes, I heard her call out my name.

"Follow my voice!" Cold air moved my hair against my cheek as the Flame whipped about and reached as high as fourteen feet. It abruptly widened and creaked like an old tree as I saw something moving inside of it. Crwys was ready just in case what came through wasn't Kathy.

But there was no need to worry. Robin's niece came tumbling out like a toddler on a long, fast slide. She did a roll on the ground and came up sitting on her backside. Wearing jeans, a Hello Kitty t-shirt, and pink sneakers, Kathy looked around at everyone and when she saw me, she yelled out, got up and came running. I held on to her hard and pulled her away from that Flame, just in case it wanted to take her back.

As we sat to the side, I realized why Arden had chosen those particular women. Each called out a child's name and coaxed them forward, brimming with love, warmth and welcome. And when the last child on the list appeared and Adrian scooped him up, Arden dismissed the Flame and staggered away.

Kyle helped her inside as we ushered the children in. I wanted to set them up in the TV room, but after recent events, I turned the flat screen on in the formal room and let them play. They all looked as if nothing had happened. Like they had been away on a play date.

When I mentioned this, Joan was the one that came up to me. "I'm a child psychologist. Children are much more resilient than we give them credit. Plus, the place where they went fed on their fears and their anger, their terror and their resentment. It kept those things when they left."

"You mean they can't feel that anymore?"

She laughed and put a hand on my arm. "Oh heavens no. They'll feel those things all too soon because our society will nurture it. But for a while, they won't."

"Right now," Crwys said as he came up beside us. "I need to come up with some plausible story as to how I found them."

"*We*, found them," Arden said as she neared. She had a coat on and a hot cup of coffee in her hand. "I have just the plan in mind, Detective, if you're up for a little direction."

I didn't want to know what they would come up with. I figured I'd read about it in the paper. That was their problem. Mine was trying to figure out the rest of the problems. Like, how was I going to get Ivan out of government custody so he could make a book? And how in the hell did Ronald Kennett turn three Witch Elders into Shadow People? I doubted he built a Coyote Flame and made them.

And though finding the children was going to look good on Arden's record, unless I could connect Kennett or someone else to the Elders's deaths, she still might be indicted.

"Sam?"

I looked down to see Kathy looking up at me. I hadn't told her about her mother yet. I didn't have the heart, and I thought that should be Robin's place, not mine. I knelt down beside her. "What is it, Kathy?"

"Is the Hat Man going to try and take us back to that place?"

"The Hat Man?"

"Yeah. The big scary guy."

"Kathy, while you were in the that other place, did you ever go visit your house?"

"I tried to. But then Hat Man found me and he threw me out," she smiled. "I saw what you did to him. You cut off his legs! You're my new hero, Sam. I wanna be just like you when I grow up!"

EIGHTEEN

Crwys, Levi and Arden, as well as her entourage, took the kids to a remote location. Somewhere Arden knew about and not a place she owned. Not even clandestinely. It was Levi's suggestion they find the kids and Arden's people would build on some story to make it plausible to the police.

How they were going to get the kids to give the same story?

Not my circus.

I know that sounded crass and flippant, but I was tired. I'd used up what juice I got from the ritual bath and needed real, unconscious sleep before I tackled getting Ivan freed so I could give the Clerics a damn copy of that book and they'd go away.

Or...so I thought.

But you know...my life was one big disaster after another lately.

Kyle drove Grey and I to the shop so I could go upstairs and pass out, remembering to set my alarm to wake up before nine, since that was my deadline.

But when I unlocked the back door to my shop the lights came on and the door was jerked open from the inside. I reached behind me for my guns, realized they were in my bag hanging over my shoulder and faced a very angry Fred the Cleric in his full robe regalia.

He pointed a very non-magical gun at me and motioned me inside. I made a clicking noise and Grey took off back down the steps. Fred moved the gun in an attempt to shoot my familiar and that's when I kicked him in the balls. I will admit...that might not have been the best time for him to piss me off. Not the way I was feeling.

I grabbed his gun, checked the ammo and set the safety, not that he'd know that and pointed it at him. "Get out of my house."

Fred writhed on the ground on his side in a fetal position, gasping for breath. It was the most dramatic display of *I just had my balls kicked* I'd ever seen. In fact…it was *way* over the top. I narrowed my eyes and sent out a few *feels* that determined very fast Fred was not the only Cleric in the shop.

I stepped inside over Fred's performance and hit the main switch to turn the lights on in the back. "You can come out. I know you're here." I went to the large table in the break room area and set my bag on top of it. I plopped in my chair and started taking my shoes off.

Emily was the first one to show up, coming from the direction of my office. Then the other two appeared. Fred…well…I could hear him sobbing. I dunno…maybe my cowgirl boots busted one of his nuts.

"That was a rather crude display," Emily said. I didn't like her tone. Especially after we'd saved her life at Arden's earlier.

"Pointing a gun at me at five in the morning is what I call crude. What do you people want? It's not nine yet. There's still time."

Miss Water, still very unique with her black hair, black lips and black nails, approached the opposite end of the table. "We heard you were with Arden tonight. We know there was a Coyote Flame made."

I leaned back after my boots were off and I could wiggle my toes. I wondered where Grey was and summoned the Sylph, with the askance to find my familiar. He smiled, kissed my cheek and disappeared.

"You have a very unique way with your Elementals."

"I don't control them. I give them space. I do what my aunt taught me."

"Your aunt being Inamorata Devonshire."

I cringed at the name, knowing what creature possessed that body. "Yeah. Look… I'm impressed you already know about the Coyote Flame. Why are you here?"

"The children taken by the Leviathan have been located," Emily said this with a less than happy inflection in her voice.

I looked at her. "Man…you guys do have sneaky snoopers everywhere. How did you know this already? Is that a bad thing?"

"It's a bad thing if someone shoved that many innocent children into a Coyote Flame. Do you realize what that could have done?"

"If left in that space, those children could have become full on badass scary Shadow People. But as it was, my associates investigated calls that came into my shop. All of them were about ghost sightings. What Ivan and Kyle saw were little Shadow People."

"And you figured this out all on your own?"

"No. It was a group effort."

"And Arden participated?"

I sat forward, really not liking this interrogation. "Can you people be a bit more forthcoming as to why you're in my home grilling me on what should be a joyous occasion? Come on…those kids are back. Unharmed."

"That will be for us to judge in the coming weeks," Emily said. She kept her Cleric robe closed around her. So did Air and Water. "What concerns us is this event now puts Arden Vervain in a positive spotlight."

"And you don't like that because you want to warlock her."

Fred appeared then, walking a little funny, and visibly mad. "Just do it and let's raise this place to the ground." His voice was pitched a little higher.

The Sylph returned and sat on my shoulder. I received an image of Grey outside near the back in the alley. Waiting. And…she wasn't alone.

There were other familiars. Or…other dogs that looked a lot like wolves.

My phone buzzed and I pulled it from my jeans. Yes. Rude. But I wasn't concerned with annoying these people. It was Pauline again and I put it to voicemail. Again. That's when I saw I had seven missed calls and six messages.

My Salamander appeared on the table in front of me, facing the Clerics. My Gnome and my Undine appeared. All of my Elementals were there. I looked at each of them, feeling a bit of panic creep up my shoulders. "I didn't summon them."

"No. I did."

This was a new voice. It was male, deep, and not at all cheery. It reminded me of Christopher Lee's voice. And when the shadows parted to my left near my office, this Cleric looked like Christopher Lee. But I recognized him.

This was Cromwell Dryden, the High Grand Master of the Witch's Parliament.

And he was in my shop.

I pushed my chair back and stood. I might not readily adhere to the magical system around me, but Ina made sure I knew it. Maybe Dionysus dreamed of this day, of me facing the most powerful of the Witches.

If so…I was fucked.

I bowed and then curtsied. I wasn't sure what I was supposed to do. "High Grand Master."

"Samantha Elizabeth Hawthorne," his commanding voice saying my name sent a shock up my spine. "The charges I've heard brought against you and Arden Vervain are most troubling. These Clerics believe Arden has the Malleus Maleficarum. And they suspect you know this to be true and are helping her hide it."

"High Grand Master—I told them yesterday—I don't believe she has it. I don't think any of us have it. I believe its location died with High Witch Higgins."

"That's just a stupid—" Fred started to say.

Dryden held up his hand and Fred stopped talking. All of my Elementals came to me, surrounded me, almost as if protecting me, yet I knew they understood this man's power. He was a full Elemental himself, with control of Spirit and three Dianic Gifts. Telekinesis, clairvoyance and psychometry. "It's a good theory. All four of you have issued reports that Higgins was less than forthcoming about his own activities. And he did not disclose the hiding place, as he was required to. But," and then he refocused on me. "I am also told a Witch and her coven are missing. Their disappearance coincides with the missing Hammer. There are those within the Parliament that wonder if there are other plots churning within."

I wasn't sure I knew what he was getting at. And it must have been evident on my face.

"Samantha, you are very much like your mother. We were devastated by her loss. And yet we were appreciative of Inamorata's volunteering to raise you. You have a strong loyalty of your Elementals. Do you sense it?"

"Yes, sir."

"They are willing to fight for you. This tells me they sense no guilt in you. Or at least, what they perceive as guilt. Elementals have a different code of morals. They are not human."

I knew this. Basic Elemental training. "Sir...I honestly don't know where the Hammer is."

"It is Parliament's suspicion Arden Vervain hid it. That she used it to set up the Changelings so that she could maneuver herself into a position of power. It is well known she seeks to be part of Parliament."

"But sir, a Leviathan created the Changelings. That same Leviathan is what put those children into that Flame."

"And you have proof of this?" he held out his hands. "Where is this Leviathan?"

And there I was—stuck between oh and fuck. I hadn't shared Inamorata's early fate with anyone but Ivan, Crwys, Levi and Kyle. Arden knew but only because it was necessary. Did I want the whole Parliament to know I'd been raised by a Leviathan? Not just any Leviathan, the very one that destroyed my mother? I knew if this was made public, a scourge would be placed on Dionysus and every available Cleric in the world would be after him. They would get to him first.

But I wanted that right.

I wanted to destroy him, banish him, and dismantle his essence myself.

"Samantha, you either don't know, or you are hiding something. I am reluctant to believe the latter, but until I have proof of such a thing, the Parliament's judgment stands as it is."

My eyes widened. "What does that mean?"

"It means you're going down," Fred said.

And then he wasn't there anymore. Just...gone.

Emily looked back and shook her head. "Crom, you just removed part of our pentagram." Her tone was conversational, but I caught the quiver at the end of her sentence. The Clerics feared this man as well.

"Not an issue. Also, I do not trust him when it comes to Eliza's child. He seems a bit more...antagonistic toward her. Do we know why?"

Mister Air cleared his throat. "We think it's because Eliza Hawthorne had his father warlocked. She apprehended him experimenting with Arcane."

What?!

"I see. Then I would instruct you to remove Fred Chadwick from your membership and bring in a new Fire Element Elder." He refocused on me and my Elementals raised their hackles. So did I.

I'm here.

I blinked at the voice. It was that woman's voice again. A voice I'd been hearing periodically since Medbh disappeared. Oh shit...was it her? Was she somehow still around and not in that magic necklace Brendi took with her?

"Samantha Elizabeth Hawthorne, it is Parliament's wish, and that of this Cleric's mission, to investigate the disappearance and reappearance of the children allegedly involved in the Changeling events before Samhain. It is also established that your constant interference in this investigation, including and pertaining to Arden Vervain, has become an impediment. It is my opinion you do not have all the facts, and though you have acted with passion and fortitude for the good of Cowen and Witch alike, you have also left a wake of rubble behind you."

I did not like the way this sounded. I felt my hands grow warm as my own defenses kicked in.

"Please do not make this difficult. I sense your exhaustion will make this easier for us, but not for you. I'm afraid for the duration of this investigation pertaining to the Malleus Maleficarum and the validation of your claims of a Leviathan's involvement, I must grant the local Cleric's request for a warlock."

It took me a second to realize—he meant *me*. I took a very voluntary step back. "But...I haven't done anything wrong. I haven't committed a crime. Warlocking is punishment for a crime!"

"You are right, Samantha. But it's been pointed out that you are one of our rare Elemental sisters and very powerful in your own right, perhaps too powerful for one who hasn't been initiated into any service. Even your mother dedicated her power to Parliament and to righting wrongs."

"I do right wrongs. I banish anything that doesn't belong in this realm."

"And who are you to be jury, judge and executioner? Samantha, you've not given any service. Therefore, your magic could prove to be harmful," he held out his hand, palm up. "If we find that you haven't been party to the theft of the Hammer, or have not plotted or schemed in any way to disrupt this Parliament then the warlock will be lifted."

If he wanted me to agree to this, it just wasn't happening. "Are you warlocking Arden as well?"

"No. She has given service several times, and if we did so now in light of the events tonight, it would look bad on our part politically."

I got it. Oh yeah...I understood then. Arden just came off smelling like a rose because she "found" those kids. I'd kept myself out of it. So if they warlocked her now, they would look like a pack of jealous old assholes bent on making the heroine look bad. "I'm the scapegoat. I'm your Azazel."

"That's a strange reference to use, but it is fitting."

"You can't do this."

"I can. And I will. If you fight...if your Elementals fight...it is not only you that will feel pain, Samantha."

This just wasn't happening to me. Me? I'd kept my shit down, I'd made sure not to cause trouble, and the first time I'm anywhere near Arden Vervain...I get warlocked?

My Elementals looked up and back at me. I looked at each of them. I didn't want them to feel pain. That wasn't our covenant together. I could fight, but I would lose. I was too tired, with no backup and no reinforcements coming.

I considered making my own Coyote Flame and jumping in... but that was just dumb. And I was pretty sure Crwys would just come after me and berate me.

Shaking my head at them, they lowered their weapons and fists. Cromwell Dryden stepped toward me, his hand still out. I lifted my own…lowered it. Lifted it… "You promise me when I'm exonerated, I'll be free."

"Yes. That is why I am here, and did not wish to leave it up to any of the local Clerics. They apparently don't like you."

"The feeling's mutual."

This man had power. Tons of it, just simmering beneath the surface like lava in the bottom of a volcano. It burned, bubbled and hummed along as I put my hand in his.

The first to go was my Salamander. He vanished and I knew, somehow I knew, Cromwell had him. The second was my Undine and I saw it in the hands of Miss Water, encased in a bubble of water. With each removed Element I felt a piece of me being ripped away like someone stabbing me in the stomach. I bent over as my Sylph was taken by Mister Air and then hidden from me.

And last I looked at Emily as she smiled and took my Gnome. The Gnome fought and Emily struck her across the face. I reacted as if I'd been slapped and Cromwell pointed at her. "You do that again, and I will warlock you. Permanently. Do I make myself clear? You are each tasked to take care of these Elementals. They are not yours. They are not to be used, forced or abused in any way. If I hear of it, then you will be disbanded and your own Elementals removed. Do I make myself perfectly clear?"

Each of them nodded, though Emily and Miss Water looked particularly miffed.

I was barely standing. My knees folded into rubber and as I sunk down and the High Grand Master took me in his arms and lifted me. There was something profoundly familiar about the sensation I had when I looked up into his eyes. He said a few words and I felt something vanish inside, like someone had shut off white noise.

And there was total and utter silence.

Pain shot up from my lower back to the base of my skull and I screamed.

Grey howled.

NINETEEN

When I was eight and my mom didn't come home, I slept for three days. No one knew why and they couldn't explain it medically. Dad couldn't wake me up. Neither could the doctors. So they assumed I'd slipped into a mystery coma.

When I did wake up, it was because Inamorata was there. She came to the hospital room and had my dad step out. He told me later he had no idea what happened, but thirty minutes afterward I was awake. I didn't ask for my mom. I asked for my dad.

And for my Aunt Ina.

Thinking back on those stories, I had to wonder if my mystery coma was something my mom induced, or I did to myself because I knew on some level she was gone. Or maybe Ina had done it—or rather Dionysus did—to weasel himself into our world.

My world.

That's what I was thinking when I woke up. Was Dionysus still pulling my strings? Was it possible this inevitable destruction of what I was, the bastard's final design? And there was always that question why? I woke that morning with no real knowledge of what my mother had been doing. No understanding of Revenants or Leviathans, Faeries or Ghouls. And as long as I didn't know the past, why would Dionysus insist on punishing the progeny?

Was there any reason at all?

When I did open my eyes in the present, the light hurt and I had to blink. My ears felt as if they were filled with cotton and when I was touched, there was this strange delay for me. It was as if I was piloting my body from a little room in my head, and I wasn't truly a part of the whole thing. That feeling slowly faded away as I stared at the fire amber eyes searching my face.

"Can you hear me? Sam? If you can understand me, please nod your head or something."

I could hear Crwys. I didn't want to nod my head because it hurt.

Everything...hurt.

I saw Kyle behind Crwys as he put his hand on the detective's shoulder. "She's been like this for twenty-four hours. She opens her eyes, she looks around, and she goes back to sleep."

Crwys sat back and I saw he was holding my hand. Shouldn't Robin be holding my hand? He was my boyfriend. I opened my mouth and asked them where Robin was. But no one answered. Then I doubted I'd opened my mouth at all.

"Is this what a warlocking is supposed to be? I want to see them, Kyle. I want to see all of them. Pluck them from their homes and pile them in a room and light it all on fire."

That thought made me smile. Or at least, I think I smiled.

"Oh like that's going to win friends," Kyle sighed. "Crwys, I hear you. But Arden said this was a command from the High Grand Master himself. He actually came to New Orleans and—"

"Effectively destroyed the only chance we have of clearing Arden's name or finding the Hammer." Crwys smoothed my hair and I watched his hand. I thought I saw an image on the inside of his wrist. It looked like a bird...a faded tattoo of a bird on fire.

At least I think it was a bird. But I knew every inch of Crwys. How had I missed a tat?

My gaze traveled from his wrist to the wall to my left, then up at the ceiling and to my right. I recognized machines, I saw tubing and I looked at Crwys again. I wasn't at home. I was in a hospital. That explained the smell.

Crwys stood, leaned down and kissed my forehead. His lips were like fire. "Just...call me if things change." He kissed my hand and turned to leave.

"Where are you going?"

"You don't need to know, Kyle."

"If you do anything that might bring attention to you—"

There was a pause and I looked down the length of the bed at them. I could see my feet sticking up under the sheets. It looked like an M.

"I'm not your concern, Kyle. Sam is. They've successfully destroyed her."

The air pressure in the room changed and I smelled perfume. A lot of it. It made me sneeze.

"….like a maniac. Never, ever let that boy behind the wheel of a car. But he had to get here. Said he knew what to do!"

It was Arden Vervain's voice.

Ivan leaned in close and put his cheek against my forehead. He sighed and I could feel him vibrating. He pressed his lips against my ear. "I know what to do. They took away the Elements, but they can't touch your power."

I liked what he said, but it didn't really make sense to me. But with his words I felt a heart breaking sadness and started crying. Or I think I did. Ivan leaned back and wiped away a tear. "Crwys…I need you to stand guard at that door. And don't let anyone in."

"Why?"

"I can't tell you. You'll have to trust me. Kyle, I need you and Arden to step outside with him."

"Like hell," Kyle said. "I don't know what you've got planned, but you've got to realize your…brand of magic's not going to undo what they did."

"No it's not," Ivan smiled. He had such a charismatic smile. That's when I realized he wasn't wearing a t-shirt with his hoodie, but a shirt with a collar. His silver lip ring shown bright under the lights as he turned to them. "Look, you're all going to have to trust me. Please. I can't tell you anything because it's not my thing to tell. It has to come from Sam."

I looked at them. Kyle, Arden and Crwys looked at each other before they filed out of the room.

"Sam, you have to listen to me. I can sort of sense what it's like for you. You're disconnected because they took your cord to this world. Well, I'm betting there's a way to give you a new one. But it'll have to be your decision."

"How are you here?" My voice sounded muffled like his and everyone else's. It sounded like I was talking through a pillow. "You were arrested…"

"That was two days ago, Sam. Jack Roberts helped clear my name."

Two…days ago? I'd been asleep for two days?

"Jack's good at what he does, and he has some pull with the people he works for. Apparently the IP that was reportedly given as being your shop was spoofed. That's the evidence Ronald Kennett sent to the cyber team. But Jack's like a forensic net person. He found the discrepancies and proved *Bell, Book and Candle* didn't even have an IP."

"So how do we get Internet?"

He winked. "Me."

Oh. Yay. Ivan was a human router too.

"The agent in charge wasn't happy when I didn't turn out to be their man, but he was good at noting Jack's logic and his skills," he grinned and winked. "I also think Jack's got a crush on Kyle. But just wait."

Ivan sat back and I watched him as he closed his eyes, held out his hands palms up and then opened his eyes. They were green now, and I knew what he was doing. And somehow…just knowing was enough for me to find the strength to push myself up on the bed.

The Hammer formed between his hands. Not in the necklace USB anymore, but in a fully formed book. One I'd become intimately acquainted with. And there was something else—

I saw his magic. How was it I'd seen his magic when I no longer had any magic of my own?

The book finished assembling and dropped into his lap. He turned it around so that it faced me and with his head bowed, placed it in my lap. "I seem to know the answer is inside this."

The book swirled with glittering red Arcane. I could still see it! I put my hand on it and the stuff came up in spirals to brush against my fingers. I felt it there, feathered brushes of a spider's web, and with each touch there was a white spark of life.

I licked my lips. "I...I shouldn't be able to see this."

Ivan looked relieved as he nodded. "I knew it the moment Arden explained what a warlocking was. It's taking way your Elemental connections, but it's not taking away your power. You've touched Arcane, Sam. I've heard all the stories of how it changes people, and it takes things away and how bad it is, but I haven't seen a single ill effect with you. So I thought...what if you could still use Arcane Magic?"

I clasped the book in my hands. It pulsed as the red magic whirled around me and my hearing didn't sound so cotton-filled and my mind wasn't so slow to comprehend and react. I opened the book and watched as the spells moved and shifted around the printed words, the only words those not anointed with the magic of Arcane would see. "You're saying I should do what I've always done, but use Arcane."

Ivan shrugged. "Why not? Sam, I've been watching it pulse around your body ever since we found you at Ina's that night with the vampire bite. Whatever it is, whatever gives it its mystical mojo or its forbidden power, it's obvious to me it resonates with you."

"But it's not supposed to work like that, is it?" My voice was my own again as my mind cleared and the final bits of fog lifted.

"Who says? The ones that can't wield it?" he put his hands on mine. "When you first told me I had to be careful about what I could do because there would be people who wouldn't understand, the problem was I didn't understand. And since then I've encountered those people and now I do understand. It's human nature to hide or suppress or destroy what they don't know."

"He's right."

Ivan whirled around as I looked past him. Crwys stood inside the room, his arms down at his sides. I narrowed my eyes at him. "That door didn't open."

"No. It didn't."

I looked at the Hammer in my hands and then looked at Ivan. "You told him."

"He already knew."

Crwys returned to my side as Ivan stepped away. "Did you think I couldn't see it, flashing around you sometimes? Did you think I couldn't sense your signature in that Circle? I have a good idea of what happened that night."

I put my hand to my mouth and fought back nausea.

"And see *that*?" he pointed at me. "That reaction right there, that sickness you feel in your soul, that's why I know it was an accident. Arcane Magic doesn't make people into killers. It just gives them the power to kill because they want to kill. But it's not in your nature."

I searched his face. "So....what? You and Ivan think I need to just use the Arcane? The Clerics will know, won't they?"

"Don't use it like you've been using magic. Use it to stay sane until your Elementals are returned. Let the Arcane keep your sanity in check," he glanced back at Ivan. "Did you tell her?"

"I was getting to it."

Crwys smiled. "Ivan's traced Ronald Kennett's location."

I looked at both of them in turn. "He's got a location? I don't understand."

"The children were tossed into that limbo world through a Coyote Flame. It created a pocket and the children never crossed over to the other side. They stayed right where they came in. They all knew instinctually the door was also the way out. But Ronald and the Elders...their situation is different."

"You know this?" I stared at Crwys.

"Don't ask how. I'll tell you one day. They came into the same limbo a different way."

"Right, they didn't come in through a Flame but through the computers?" Ivan asked.

"No. Not even that. They came in without bodies."

I pushed back into the pillows. Oh...damn. I hadn't even considered that. Of course. The kids were put in with their physical bodies. They had vehicles to travel in and out. But Ronald died while in Cyberspace. That limbo between living and dying. "Did he lure the Elders to him?"

"I think he tricked them in some way. He definitely killed them so they could get in the way he did. So when that didn't work and using the kids didn't work when they showed up, I think Ronald started looking or for other means. He learned about the Malleus Maleficarum. He wanted that book. I assume he learned about how entities in other worlds possess human bodies, like Daemons, Revenants, Leviathans, Succubus, Incubus..."

"And he thought he could do the same. With the old men," Ivan gave a long sigh. "If I were going to possess a body, I would not want an old man body."

"It was the magic that attracted him," Crwys glanced at Ivan. "The Arcane in them. Those old men had messed with Arcane before." He smiled. "I checked their graves, and the urn one of them is cremated in."

I smiled at him. "You could see it."

"And I think, or suspect, Ronald found you somehow, sensed the Arcane and wanted your body."

Putting my hand to my neck, I thought about the Shadow in the shop. "But he never attacked me."

"As a Witch, you weren't vulnerable."

"But now he thinks I am," I hissed. "That bastard set me up to get warlocked."

"I would almost count on it," Crwys pushed back and stood next to Ivan. "I think they're going to try something stupid to get your attention and they're going to try and lure you to them."

I watched Ivan. "You already know this is true."

"Which is why we have to move on Ronald and his band of three nasty old men before he comes at you. Ronald has to have a home base, a place he can draw power from. And Ivan found that place in a residence in Picayune, Mississippi. It could be a home computer with a good sized hard drive with a lot of empty space—"

All of those calls from Pauline suddenly took on a greater importance. Dad talking to something in the house. Dad begging Pauline to call me because I could exorcise their home.

I threw the sheets off of myself and slid out of bed, not caring if my bare ass was visible to anyone in the room. I didn't feel the dizziness I felt before when Cromwell took my Elementals. Instead I felt stronger. I willed the Hammer to revert to the charm and it did, with no spoken command. I put it around my neck. "Where's my phone?"

"It's with your things in that bag over there," Ivan pointed to the chair.

I grabbed the bag and dumped it out on the bed. My phone bounced to the right and I grabbed it, unlocking it immediately. There were three more missed calls, all from Pauline, all from yesterday. Nothing since. I redialed the last call and waited.

No answer. It didn't even flip to voicemail.

I played the messages. All of them said about the same thing. *"Sam, I really, really need you to call us back here. There is something in this house and it's got your father all worked up. He's scaring me, and if you can't get here I'm going to have to call the doctor."*

I tried my dad's landline.

The old answering machine picked up and I waited for the beep. "Dad it's Sam, can you pick up? If you don't know where my voice is coming from, it's the phone in the corner. The blue one."

I felt Crwys's and Ivan's eyes on me. I'd never told anyone about my dad's condition.

When he didn't pick up, I hung up and called Pauline's cell phone again.

This time it went to voicemail.

"Sam why did you call your dad?" Ivan said.

I stared at my phone. "What's the address you traced Kennett to?"

Ivan repeated it.

Crwys cursed under his breath.

"What?" Ivan said.

I turned and looked at him and it took a lot not to cry. "That's my dad's address."

TWENTY

Crwys drove a '64 Mustang Fastback. It was in cherry condition, but it couldn't carry everyone. Five comfortably. After an abrupt departure from the hospital, with yells of more tests, we got to *Bell, Book and Candle* in record time. The weather at least had cleared up a bit. Scattered clouds moved over the sky, throwing shadows on the winter morning. The temperature was in the lower fifties, which was cold for the South.

I ran upstairs and changed clothes, refusing to look at the break room, the scene of my incarceration. I wasn't sure I could ever go back into that room without suffocating when I thought of the looks on my Elementals' faces. I worried about them, how they were being treated, if they were being misused or neglected, and decided it didn't matter what sort of heinous crimes a Witch committed—punishing the Elementals was not acceptable. It wasn't their fault.

New jeans, tank top, shirt and jacket, new socks and then boots. The Hammer buzzed against my chest, warm and almost comforting. I felt good. *Really* good. And powerful, even though I shouldn't. Not with my essence capped.

Once I had everything I needed, I went down the stairs and heard the others talking in the break room. I stopped where I was and listened. I didn't snoop normally, but when I heard my name mentioned, I reacted.

"…normal. This is dangerous shit here." That was Kyle. "I don't care if it seems right or feels right to her. She shouldn't be using Arcane."

"I just want to know how she's using it. *Shugar*, I got all kinds of horror stories in my family of members trying to make that shit work. The results will curl your hair," Arden said.

"Arcane or not, what's dangerous is there is a Shadow Asshole still out there with a vendetta against me and Sam," Ivan sounded angry. I'd never heard that tone from him before.

"Why would this dead person have a vendetta against Sam?" Arden asked.

"Why else zero in on her dad's home?" Levi chimed in. "I'm gonna go with Ivan on this one. The kids are safe, and Arden came out smelling like a rose while Sam, who put all this together, got warlocked. That's not fair."

"Life's not fair."

"Bitch, you need to show a bit more respect."

"You need to take care who you're talking to, Leech," Arden's tone hardened.

The level of discord they were creating unnerved me. I needed help getting to my dad's house and I needed a bonded team working together to rid the world of Ronald Kennett. I closed my hand around the USB at my neck and felt the surge of power, of adrenaline.

Two weeks ago, I'd run off and tried to solve my own problem with the Leviathan because everyone had been taken from me. Now, when I thought I had everyone's support, I realized I didn't when I really, really needed them.

I wasn't sure how I was going to kill this son of a bitch. I just knew I had to. And I didn't need a moral contingent keeping me back. I quietly moved back up the stairs and out to the veranda that spanned the length of the building overlooking Bourbon Street. My Jeep was parked in back so I climbed down the fire escape.

Hands grabbed my hips as my boots touched the ground and I spun to see Crwys smiling at me. "What are you doing?"

"Making sure you don't do something stupid on your own."

"I'm not going back in there. Half of them don't trust me just because of the Arcane."

He glanced over at his car where Grey stuck her head out the driver's window. "Grey and I have confidence in you. We're just not going to let you go by yourself."

"It's an hour or so drive."

"I'm a cop."

And Crwys used that to his advantage. Once we hit the expressway, he set a flashing light on his dashboard. "I have a price for this."

I rolled my eyes. Figured.

"You tell me everything. And I mean everything. What *really* happened in Ina's house? And don't say nothing, because you forget Ivan and I were the ones to find you."

"I'm surprised he didn't come with you."

Crwys grinned. Dear Lady he had the cutest dimples when he did that. "Me meeting you at the fire escape was his idea." He reached into his jacket pocket and handed me a note.

I opened it and read Ivan's scrawled type.

Get out there and go with her. This group's not ready to help her, not the way you can. They can't see past their own fears and prejudices to realize Sam's got something different going on. I don't know what it is. Maybe you do. I'll stay here and create the copy she wanted. When you save her dad and stepmom, come back and we can work on hiding the book in a place the Clerics can find it. That should be enough for them to remove the warlock.
And take Grey. You two should really come clean about the truth.
I

I held the note out. "What truth? What's he talking about?"

Crwys touched the note and it evaporated. Just turned to ash and disappeared. Damn I hated when he did that. "I have no idea what he's talking about. Just know that Ivan's going to get us the prop we need to clear you and Arden. He's also going to work on clearing up planted evidence out there."

"How?"

"You concentrate on telling me what I asked for."

"What about Levi?"

"He and I are in constant communication. He knows what I'm doing."

I had no idea what that meant.

The drive took just under an hour with Crwys driving like a crazy person cop. I told him everything that happened that night, from getting back to the house and thinking Ina was a Ghoul, to the reality of what I'd done when I killed Arwen and learning Ina wasn't one of Dionysus's Ghouls, but the Leviathan himself. Ina had been that very Leviathan all those years, hiding quietly and patiently in my life, invisible to everyone.

"Because Medbh removed Ina's soul." Crwys's jaw worked a bit as I watched him. Grey's head rested on my left shoulder where she stuck her head between the front seats. "Even I didn't realize what she was. I mean Levi and I always sensed she was powerful, but I just thought that was a Witch thing."

I watched him for a while as we entered Picayune city limits and he slowed the car down. "You don't hate me?"

He glanced at me and I moved back. His brows knitted together over his nose and his eyes were red. "Hate you? That bastard tricked you. Groomed you. Hell, he had a spell woven into the simplest of tasks just to find out everything you knew every day."

He was talking about the peeling of apples. All those years I peeled apples for Ina's pies and told her about my day, what I did, whom I talked to, and what I said…and never realizing until that night two weeks ago that Ina never made an apple pie. "It doesn't change the way I feel about myself."

"If you didn't feel guilt, then I *would* be mad at you. You wouldn't be human. That's what makes you special to me." He turned the car down all the right roads until we came up on the two-story my dad bought after he and Pauline married. Their cars were still in the driveway and it looked like Pauline had started putting up Christmas decorations before Thanksgiving arrived. That hideous plastic snowman was out by the porch steps and red glittery garland, much like Arcane Magic, was wound around the porch support beams.

All three of us piled out of the car and approached the house. I retrieved my Smith & Wessons as Crwys pulled his Desert Eagle out of its holster. We came up the drive to the garage and I punched in the code. The garage door opened with a loud, grinding sound.

"So much for the element of surprise," Crwys quipped.

"It's not a surprise," I said. "If Kennett's in there, then he's in the house's security system. See the cameras? He already knows we're here."

I absently tried to send out my *feels* and realized... I couldn't. I wanted to call up my Elementals and knew they couldn't hear me. I was really on my own on this. No magic crutch. No way of exorcising this asshole if I found him at all.

I had Arcane. Big deal? They were just spells in a book crunched down into microscopic bytes of data in a USB around my neck. How was I supposed to fight something like Kennett? I wasn't a Cyber Witch like Ivan. I couldn't grab kitchen herbs and bind an enemy like a Hedge Witch.

Why was I here? I could shoot a flea off an armadillo's back, but bullets were useless against Shadows.

Crwys and I quietly moved to the door in the garage. This door would lead into the kitchen, then into a private den and the dining room. Pauline had moved Dad into the downstairs bedroom because it made it easier to manage him when he had one of his episodes. I noticed the bars on the kitchen door window as I removed my key from my back pocket and unlocked the door.

The instant I opened the door I smelled it. No other thing in the world had that scent.

Blood.

Crwys put his hand up to stop me from bolting in. He signaled me to move in behind him. He held his weapon in front of him and quietly, slowly, moved into the house. I was close behind him, my weapons pointed down so I didn't shoot him in the back.

The house was still and the smell was overwhelming. Fear crept along my shoulders as we moved from the kitchen to the three-door portal. The door in front of us went to the private den, the door to the right opened into the dining room, and the door on the other side of that room opened into the front hall and the front door.

I gestured with my left hand and gun to the den. That's where my dad hung out with Pauline most days.

He nodded slowly and stepped in through the door.

The moment I put my foot through the threshold, I knew.

I knew because I saw her bloody hand sticking out from between the couch and coffee table. I gasped. Crwys sighed as he moved around and looked at me. He could see the whole room. "Sam…don't…"

But I was already moving further in. My stare focused on Pauline's hand and traveled down her arm to her dark hair. She lay face down on the carpet, a dozen or so splotches of blood on her back, bleeding into the fabric of her blouse. Her skin was gray and I knew before Crwys bent down to press his fingers at her neck, Pauline Hawthorne was dead.

Another woman in teddy bear scrubs lay on her side, just past the couch. Her dark skin was ashen in death. Blood soaked through the cartoon bears, marring their happy smiles. This was probably the new nurse Pauline said they hired.

I sensed what was just past the nurse. Maybe I'd caught a glimpse of it when I looked around. Maybe it was just an image from a nightmare. I didn't want to look, but I had to.

There was no going back.

Dad sat in his favorite chair by the fireplace. It gave him an excellent view of the new flat screen I'd bought them last Christmas. His mouth was open in a silent scream below wide eyes that stared at something terrifying. In his right hand he held the hilt of a knife. The blade was buried in his chest.

I brushed past Crwys and I dropped to my knees beside my dad's chair. I half dropped, half set the guns on the floor and tentatively touched his neck. I knew before I did that he was dead. Been dead. It was evident in the white film over his eyes and the sticky blood coating his chest and shirt. I heard whimpering noises and thought Grey was beside me. I realized I was the one making them as I pawed at his arm and then took his other hand in mine and pressed it against my face.

There is nothing, I think, more devastating than losing a parent. Parents may say the opposite when losing their child. But I had no real memory of my mother. My father had been my world for so long, even when he buried himself in his work and turned his affections toward Pauline. I'd still loved him.

I'd always loved him. He was all I had. The only family I knew.

There were more of those noises and I felt Crwys's warm hand on my arm. "Sam—"

"Stay away from me!" I yelled and slapped him away. He wasn't going to take me away from my dad.

My daddy.

I moved up from my knees and touched his head, his cheek, his neck, but every contact repeated the same thing to me. He was gone. Deal with it.

Just deal with it, Sam.

"Sam…I need to call this in to the locals. It looks like he stabbed your stepmom, that nurse…and then himself."

"No!" I jumped up and struck Crwys hard across the face. I wasn't in control anymore. I was an exposed, raw nerve, bleeding out beside my dead parent. "No! He did not kill her!"

I wouldn't look at him. I couldn't look at him. I kissed my father's cheek. I wanted to scream. I wanted to…

What I wanted couldn't happen.

It wasn't possible.

And when Crwys started laughing, I grabbed one of my guns and put it in his face. "Stop it."

But Crwys wasn't the one laughing.

He reached up and pushed the barrel of the Wesson away. "Sam, I need you to get a grip. We're not alone."

The laughter deepened and I looked at my dad, and then at Pauline's body. It was the same laugh I'd heard at Ina's that afternoon, the voice of the Uncola man. But it also sounded…mechanical. Tin-like. As if it were coming through a speaker.

That's when I spotted the TV speakers. There was one on the mantel, one on a bookshelf near the door, and one at a destroyed computer in the back of the room. I slowly pivoted to look at the computer and a shadow moved across the wall.

Shit!

"Look out!" I screamed.

TWENTY ONE

I dove at Crwys as the Shadow blurred and ran toward him. It brushed my arm and froze my skin as Crwys and I went down between the fireplace hearth and the coffee table at my dad's feet.

"Mother fucker," Crwys said as he sat up and looked around the room. "We know it's you Ronald. You're in the Hawthorne hard drive."

"Of course it's me," came a computer-generated voice through the speakers. "But I'm Soul Machine now. I am a soul, in the machine!" He laughed again.

"Why did you kill my parents?" I stood, slapping at Crwys's hands trying to keep me on the floor.

"Oh…they killed themselves. It was easy to drive your dad insane. He was already halfway there, Samantha. I never knew Witches were real until I started searching for whatever it was that hacked my machine. It left no footprint. No signature. Not even an IP. Nothing."

"That was Ivan."

"Yes…" The Shadow reappeared on the back wall. It looked like it did that day in Ina's kitchen. Like a man with no detail. Except it was much, much shorter. Its legs were truncated, a third the length of its arms. Crwys stood and we both faced it. "Ivan. But I didn't find him till he revealed himself, and by then I knew about the Malleus Maleficarum. The real deal. A book that could give me back my body."

Crwys made a rude noise. "That's not going to happen, Ron. Your body is dead. You neglected it."

"I AM SOUL MACHINE!"

146

I narrowed my eyes and snarled at the wall image. "You are nothing but a piece of forgotten shit, you son of a bitch. You killed three men trying to get out of the machine, Ron. You thought those old men were your ticket. Realized you were pretty much pointless in there so you slaughtered three more innocent lives. You're sick. You should be put down. Erased like erroneous data. Garbage in, garbage... *out.*"

The Shadow came at me. I fired off a few rounds; bullets couldn't hit Shadows but they made nice holes on the opposite wall, smashing one of Pauline's paintings.

Bullets might not be able to strike the Shadow, but he was solid enough to shove me against the fireplace and knock the wind out of me. I fell to the floor and when Crwys tried to help me up, the Shadow knocked him backwards, crashing into the TV and onto the floor.

Before I could right myself, something grabbed me around the neck and squeezed. I looked to see the Shadow, no longer a two dimensional aberration against a wall, but three-dimensional and choking the shit out of me. I grabbed at my neck as I scrambled on the ground, trying to kick the thing in the back. But it wasn't solid! I couldn't put my fingers around anything and my knees came up and through the thing.

Again I cried out for my Elementals. I tried to summon my Spirit. They hadn't taken that! But it wasn't answering. It was too weak and needed the other Elements to fully form. I was helpless and losing my vision as I gasped for breath.

The Hammer pulsed once against my chest. I felt it ripple out through the house and under my back. The world turned red and I thought it was blood over my eyes. But it sparkled and glittered as it lowered a filter over my vision. I looked through it at the Shadow and saw a kid. A skinny, terrified, insane child filled with rage and anger. I saw the make up of his soul as it glittered bright and pure, and then began to decay. Dark, rotting patches of it fell away and I knew I was watching what it was, to what it was becoming.

The warnings about Shadow People and what they were. Bundles of emotions. A forgotten son. Left to die by parents who didn't even bother to call while they were off vacationing. A kid that never fit in. A kid that never had power, until today.

And then I saw my dad through the Shadow's eyes. I saw him yelling and screaming at something Pauline couldn't see. I saw him grab the knife and try to stab at it—over and over until he realized he'd stabbed the nurse. Pauline tried to take the knife and he stabbed her too. She staggered away to the door, barely making it to the couch before she fell to the ground.

I watched as light came back to my dad's eyes and he was himself in those last seconds as he realized what he'd done. Despair washed over him as he sat in that chair and stabbed himself until he couldn't pull the knife back out.

And through it all, I heard the Shadow's laughter.

Laughter at horror. Laughter at what it had done. A final revenge against the Witch that took the children from him. Oh yes…he'd had plans for those children once he figured out how to control them. Manipulate them.

And then I took a long hard look at the Shadows legs and saw the bloody stumps of where my Gnome axed and removed its shins and feet. The thing was in pain.

And it wanted to cause pain.

I saw it all in seconds as the Hammer's power, a power that now settled inside my blood, showed me what I could do. It instructed me on how I could easily, so…very easily…take the Shadow down to its base elements. I reached up and with a single touch, made it disappear. I heard Ronald Kennett's screams as he felt every painful, agonizing separation of every molecule of his body. The body is made up of billions of pieces, an infinite universe.

He would be screaming for a very, very long time.

I saw my father's body. He was no longer there. The vessel began its decay. I sat up and reached out for it. Touched my father's knee. Bid my creator a farewell as it disintegrated. I pushed up and touched the chair. That too fell away and then Pauline's body vanished. The nurse's body. I could see the make up of every thing in the room, the house, the yard and the neighborhood. I could erase the place of my greatest pain!

There would be nothing!

No reminder of where my father died! No house to stand and suffer through another family. I could just banish it all.

A movement in the doorway caught my attention. At first I thought it was Grey. Beautiful Grey. I beckoned her to join me. We could both disappear together in this red haze of peace. But it wasn't my wolf. It was a woman, dressed in a dated business suit, with dark hair and a familiar face. She came to me, held out her hand and spoke to me.

"Let it go, Sam. You can control it."

I didn't know what she meant. Control what?

"Sam, if you don't stop, if you don't use your Spirit to cap the power, it will destroy you, me, Crwys, everyone. Please...stop."

Spirit. I had called upon Spirit. But it wasn't strong enough. Until I summoned it again. The red haze faded as the glitter dimmed. It didn't want to do that.

An angel came into view. He was magnificent, with his golden skin, red amber eyes and leather wings. He wore nothing as he held his hand out to me.

Come back.

Was this my Spirit?

And then it was gone. A blink. A breath. A gasp. A stumble. A reawakening of color and smell. Of sound and taste. I stumbled and fell into Crwys's arms. He stood where the angel had been and his eyes were the same.

"Samantha," he said as he looked into my eyes. "I've been alive for a very, very long time. But you are the first human who has ever scared the hell out of me."

I shivered at him. I was cold. Wind brushed my hair against my cheek and I looked around the living room.

But there was no living room. No house.

We were standing in an empty lot.

We need to go. The neighbors are going to start looking out their windows.

"I know," Crwys picked my guns up off the pine straw ground and put his hands on my shoulders. "Are you with me, Sam?"

"Where…where is Dad's house?" I looked around. I recognized the lot. I knew the house across the street. I was shaking now, but not from cold. "Crwys…where is my dad's god damn house?"

Grey barked.

But I heard, *Get her in the car!*

I looked at my familiar. I looked at the lot as Crwys led me away to his car. We piled back in and he urged me to put on my seat belt as he backed the car out of the concrete drive, the only thing left of what had once been my father's house. He turned the car down a side road as I heard sirens behind us. I turned to see cop cars arriving.

"I did that," I turned back around. "I remember…Kennett's dead."

"Kennett is in hell. A hell you put him in," Crwys glanced at me. "I can't say I'm sad about it."

"I…" with a look at my hands I stumbled over the memories. "I touched my dad and Pauline."

"Sam…I think what just happened, is what all the lessons your people taught you about Arcane Magic are for."

I leaned back in the seat. Pressed myself into the vinyl cushion. *Arcane Magic will change you. It will take things from you. Arcane Magic doesn't belong in this world.*

It was all true. This was what I'd been warned about. I'd obliterated my father's house, his body, Pauline's body, the nurse, and everything in it. And I could remember the cold, calculating method I'd used to do it. I hadn't felt anything. Except…satisfaction.

I grabbed at the USB around my neck, but the necklace wasn't there. I looked around the car and grabbed at the dashboard. "We have to go back. The Hammer came off the chain. It's not around my neck."

But he didn't turn around. He glanced at me and shook his head. "It didn't fall off, Sam. It's still there."

I put my hands to my chest. But there was nothing there.

He pointed to the rearview mirror.

I pulled the mirror down to look as I leaned over.

There…in the center of my chest was a tattoo of a combined symbol, the hermetic representations of the Elements, all surrounded by a circle. "What…the hell is this?"

"I don't know, Sam," he looked straight ahead. "I just don't god damn know."

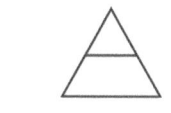

TWENTY TWO

I went crazy for a little while. Not like straitjacket crazy. This was something that happened inside. I avoided everyone for a few weeks. I spent Yule alone in my apartment. Crwys kept Grey and I closed the shop. He offered to pay the rent and utilities until I got my shit together.

But I wasn't sure that was ever going to happen.

Ivan called every day. He left me vlogs in my email. Kyle sent me hand-written letters and I could see the magic as it swirled around each one. They were reaching out.

I was pulling back.

Crwys was the only one that really left me alone. He didn't visit or write. But I had the feeling he was there.

I tried to have the tattoo removed. But nothing the artist did worked.

I even poured acid over it.

It burned like holy hell and when I finally recovered from that pain, it was still there. Not a mark on me.

I followed the news. Arden Vervain was exonerated of all charges, and even got an apology. Ronald Kennett's death was ruled a tragic accident and the deaths of the three Elders...were a mystery. I was pretty sure they were filed under cold case and were forgotten by New Year's.

Robin finally called New Year's Eve. Apologized for being distant and asked about my dad's disappearance. The house and the two elderly people that lived there made national news. Funny how they never tried to contact me. I thought maybe Arden, Crwys or even Parliament had something to do with that.

We decided to put our relationship on hold. He was busy trying to establish a new life for the girls. I could hear how happy he was that Kathy had been found. We admitted we loved one another and promised to talk again soon.

After he disconnected, I held up my glass of wine and toasted him a rich and wonderful life.

I heard the footsteps first. I was sitting on my couch in my living area. It was a half hour before midnight, before the ball dropped in New York City. I had it on my flat screen. Booze on the coffee table, along with an assortment of MSG laced Chinese food from a few doors down.

I knew who it was even before I heard Grey woof. It was so good to see her and I hugged her as she jumped on the couch and licked my face.

Crwys looked good. He wore his usual shirt, leather jacket, jeans and boots and had nice glasses in one hand and a bottle of Dom Pérignon in the other. "I figured no one should be alone on New Year's."

"Not even Samantha the destructor."

"Not even you." He grinned at me as he set the glasses and bottle on the coffee table and took his jacket off. He slung it on a chair and took the spot to my right. Grey made her big old self comfortable between us. He unwrapped the foil from the cork and held his hand over it as he pried it loose. It popped and champagne gushed out. He poured it into the two glasses and handed me one.

"It's not the new year yet. We've still got twenty minutes."

"I know. I wanted to toast you, Sam. You've had two shit months. Devastating news. And you've lived through it."

I held up the glass, we clinked and I downed half of it. "Wow. That's good. So, any word on my warlocking?"

"Arden said Parliament is torn. The majority wants it lifted with a yearlong commitment of service. Apparently they want you as a Tracker, like your mother was. But as she reminded me and the boys, they're also a bit long at making up their mind."

"So I could be like this for another day, or a year."

"Yeah. But at least you won't suffer the consequences of what a warlocking does."

I swirled the glass. "No...I just have to make sure I don't lose control again and make the entire city of New Orleans disappear."

"You won't do that."

"You don't know that."

"I do. Grey and I both do."

"Crwys...an entire house disappeared and three bodies. What does that make me?"

"It makes you human. Your despair, anger and sadness handled it the only way it knew how. It was the first time you used the magic."

"No. I killed with it. Maybe that's all the magic knows how to do."

"I don't know. What I do know is that Grey and I have something to tell you. We've talked about it long and hard and she feels it's time for you to know the truth."

Truth. I sat forward. "Is this that truth Ivan mentioned in that note?"

"What note?"

I punched him before I put my hand on Grey's back. "What do you two want to tell me?"

That I can talk.

I was smiling when the voice came to my mind. I thought it was Crwys but his lips didn't move. And I'd seen him try and throw his voice before. He sucked at it. "Wait...that's the same voice I've been hearing now and then."

Because sometimes I can't help myself. I want to protect you and well, you're pig-headed like your father was.

I looked at Grey. She was looking up at me. "You...you're talking to me."

Yes.

"You've been able to talk all this time."

Yes.

I looked at Crwys. "And you knew this?"

"She and I spoke the day I met you. But she wanted me to keep it a secret."

"Why?" I put my hands on Grey's face and turned her long nose to me. "Why would you keep such a wonderful thing a secret?"

Because I'm not supposed to be here. Keeping others in the dark as to my existence is essential.

"I'm not following."

And that's okay, Sam-Sam. As long as I'm with you, can be here to protect you, watch you grow up, that's all I've ever wanted.

I stared at Grey. Hard. She'd called me Sam-Sam. Only one person had ever...ever called me that.

My eyes burned as I thought back over what I'd learned, what I knew about Faerie lore, about taking humans on the Wild Hunt. I remembered Arden's threat that she would not be Brendi's dog.

Crwys put a hand on my shoulder. "Go on. It's okay."

I heard cheers somewhere and realized the big, jeweled ball had dropped in Times Square. The pop and crash of fireworks lit up the New Orleans sky as I stared into Grey's human-like eyes.

Was it possible? All this time? Here I thought I'd lost my entire family and I learn at the start of the new year, I'm not alone.

"Only one person ever called me Sam-Sam."

Yes.

"You were there, in the Arcane veil."

I was.

I brushed a tear from my cheek as Grey licked at my nose. I wrapped my arms around her warm, soft neck. "Mom!"

ELEMENTAL MOON
CHAPTER ONE

"You're kidding, right?" I gave my best friend and business partner my well-done *this-is-ridiculous* face, given our current situation. "Werewolves are *myths*."

Kyle Kendrick gave me his best version of the same face, which was visible in the flickering light of our waning fire. It was the beginning of January, just a few days into the new year. The moon overhead was full, which might account for the fact I could clearly see him as well as our other group member Ivan Westerfield, and my wolf familiar and mother, Grey.

Yes. That beautiful gray and white wolf is my mom. Deal. I had to.

After a two night drunkfest immediately following New Year's spent with my ex, I decided we, the Witches, needed to get back to the structure of ritual in our daily lives. So, I looked at a calendar and saw the full moon was coming up. Seemed like a great plan for us to center our energies and for me to get used to a whole new version of magic I wasn't happy with. Mom gave me a few pointers on full moon rituals, which were technically already written down in her Book of Shadows. But that book was at my Aunt Ina's house, a woman who wasn't really my aunt but a Vampire. And not just a plain Vampire, but a Leviathan Vampire. She wasn't there, having recently absconded with a soul whose body I had killed. I'd also just discovered the gardens of that house were full of dead bodies. Victims my so-called aunt had lured to her home, fed and then proceeded to go all *Hansel and Gretel* on.

While I was in high school.

Think this might be a lot to take in? You should see what it's like from my side of things. My name is Samantha Hawthorne. I'm a Witch, or I was a Witch, until the High Grand Master muckity-muck of the Witch's Parliament, or whatever they called themselves, decided I had something to do with the disappearance of a well-known Grimoire of sorts. A book known as the Malleus Maleficarum, or the Witch's Hammer. I call it the Hammer, cause the damn thing recently crushed my life.

I lost my connection to the Elements, something that made me who and what I was, but I'd gained an uncanny ability to use what is known as Arcane Magic. This is magic that has been forbidden for Witches to use for as long as I can remember. Most of the bad guys my group and I fight come from the realms where this magic thrives.

Including my ex...who might not be my ex...though I don't know.

Head spinning yet?

Good. Now pay attention.

"Guys," Ivan said as he moved in closer to us so we formed a three-backed triangle. I'm sure we looked pretty impressive. I had my hands out, my fingers laced with bright red smoky glitter. Ivan's hands were out in front, sparking with greenish electricity. And Kyle's hands, tattooed with two of the Elemental Symbols, glowed with bright yellow on his right for Air and brilliant blue on his left for Water. We were each ready to whammy anything that came at us. "Can we focus on the fact we're surrounded by a circle of really big wolves?"

He was right. Thus, the current situation I alluded to earlier.

The temperature was chilly, given it was January in Louisiana, and I could see our breath in the moonlight. Sometimes, but not this time, it dipped below freezing and made the news. I always wondered if the cause wasn't global warming related but Ceremonial Magician induced. They liked screwing up the weather. I wore my ex's leather jacket, 'cause mine had a hole in it and still reeked of Arcane taint.

Which had the aroma of two-day rotten chicken.

This jacket smelled like Detective Crwys Holliard. My ex. A fine piece of law enforcement who possessed the power of a flamethrower. Species? Unknown.

Grey sat at my side, panting, not even the least bit worried our full moon ritual had been interrupted by *lycanis humongous*. In fact, when I'd tried to talk to her, she's abruptly said, *Sshh!* in my head.

The larger of the circle lumbered forward. I didn't know if that was the right word to use, but he didn't pounce, run or attack, so lumbered seemed right. His fur looked red in the moonlight, shadowed by darker hues of auburn and orange. His eyes glowed yellow as he approached—*me!*

Grey finally stood on all fours. I'd always thought of her as large. I obviously had no real appreciation of how big wolves could get. Next to Big Red there, mom looked like a puppy.

The two touched noses, then actually moved their heads as if to entwine their necks. I looked at Kyle, he looked at Ivan and Ivan looked at us.

"Is that normal?" Ivan whispered.

I lifted my shoulders in a shrug and finally prodded her thoughts again. *Mom? What is going on? Are they going to eat us?*

She finally answered me but there was something else in the thoughts...like an echo. *No, silly. They're here because they were drawn to your magic.*

Which magic? Ours combined or you mean my—

Your Arcane. They sensed it just before the new year and again after in these very woods. The last time it appeared, four days ago, two of their own vanished. When you activated yours tonight, they were drawn here. To you.

I gulped. *You did tell him that wasn't me, right? That I'm not responsible for missing wolves? And that you're my mom?*

He knows, Sam-Sam. Your Arcane doesn't have the same smell. And yes, he knows I'm your mother. I swear I heard an echo of laughter when she said that. *Her* laughter.

I relayed what she said to the other two.

Kyle's grin was infectious. "That's just so cool that you can talk to her like that."

It would be cooler if we weren't surrounded by wolves. All of them sat back on their haunches at once. Half of them panted with their tongues out and looked about as dangerous as a circle of puppies.

Really *BIG* puppies.

Everyone sat but Big Red. He continued to stand as mom turned to look at me. *You can put your weapons away.*

Oh. I lowered my hands and snuffed out the Arcane I'd powered up. Kyle clapped his hands and their lights extinguished. Ivan knelt down and pressed his hands to the ground, releasing the electricity into the earth. Once that was done we all turned to face Big Red.

Mom spoke to me. *The Aces wish to ask a task of you, by right of the Goddess Arduinna, to which all Lycans bow.*

That…was an epic line. I delivered it to the other two, though I was sure it didn't have the same impact as my mom's internal voice.

Ivan said, "Werewolves worship the moon?"

"Lycans. They prefer to be called Lycans," Kyle said. "The moon controls shifts between the apogee and the perigee."

Ivan and I *stared* at Kyle with wide eyes.

He looked back at us as if we'd each grown two heads. "What?"

"How do you know about apogee and perigee?" Ivan asked. "I had to Google that myself when you guys started talking about a full moon ritual. And how do you know what they prefer to be called?"

Mom cleared her throat in my mind. *Kyle has something he needs to tell both of you. But now's not the time.* When she said that, I didn't hear an echo. I assumed the echo meant she was sharing the thought, and for whatever reason she didn't want Kyle's secret shared. I felt I needed to answer the request so I looked at each of them and arched my brows in question. Do we help? Or do we get eaten?

When they both nodded, I turned back to mom and Big Red. "What is the task?"

Do you accept?

"Not until we hear the task. I don't want to promise them something I don't know if I can deliver."

Mom turned and looked up at Big Red who moved in front of me; his head nearly level with my own. Grey barked several times, but

Big Red turned and gave her one hell of a roar. I jumped. So did she. It hurt watching mom take a few steps back, her ears down, whining like a wounded pup. So I started to call up a nice fireball to singe the big dog's ass off.

I wasn't prepared for what this bastard did next.

I froze as he stood up on his back legs, put his paws on my shoulders and bit into my shoulder. The whole action took less than a second. In my defense, I wasn't just standing there like some fragile deer waiting to be slaughtered. I had my mom's voice in my head saying, *Just be still. Don't move. Just be still.*

Naturally, I yelled out when he bit me. I assumed Kyle and Ivan moved or did something behind me because the wolves stood and growled low as they positioned themselves between us and the boys.

"What the hell?" Kyle called out. "You're gonna turn her into a Lycan!"

Uh. Whut?

The large wolf with his teeth buried into my shoulder blurred in front of me. The trees in the clearing spun around me as the wolf's warm fur was replaced by something softer, yet firmer. I stood with my head back, afraid to move because I didn't want my neck ripped out, and afraid to blast this son of a bitch into next year because my mom was in my head telling me everything was okay and I needed to relax. It was just a formality.

Getting bitten by a wolf was a formality?! Appetizer maybe, but…

Kyle whistled. Ivan swore.

Hands took my upper arms, just below my shoulders, and held me in a firm grip as Big Red pulled his teeth out and began licking the wound. I slowly became aware Big Red wasn't Big Red anymore. The wolf was gone, and in his place was a man. And the licking, though weird, made the pain go away.

When he stopped slobbering on my shoulder, he straightened. I looked up into the most handsome face I'd seen under a head full of red hair. The hair cascaded over his shoulders to his very bare nipples. A look down and I saw that Big Red the wolf was now Big Red the naked man.

I felt a full on body blush start from my forehead all the way to my feet. I was pretty sure if someone used a heat sensitive camera on me, I'd be flaming.

He put a very warm hand against my cheek. "*Trés belle, chérie.*" His voice was pure sex in a rich, Acadian accent. "Now *d'accord?*"

Oh my. "What…what did you just do?"

"He bit you," Kyle said from behind me. "Now you're going to become a Lycan."

"No," Big Red the naked man said. "She will not become my mate unless she breaks her promise."

"Promise?" I was getting my common sense back. Slowly. "What—I didn't make a promise. And what do you mean mate? I'm not your mate." I looked down at Grey standing beside Big Red, facing me. "What the hell? I said I wanted to hear the task first!"

I know. And I told him not to. But he thinks the best way for you to understand is to be a part of the pack. Temporarily, of course.

"Part of the pack?"

I caught a weird buzzing in my head and wasn't sure where it was coming from. Abruptly, my ears popped like they usually did in a plane and a crowd of voices filled the silence. I grabbed my ears at the volume and tried to block it out.

<Sister Mother Sorcière help attack us find them help us youhavetofindthem…thechildthechildthechild.>

The sheer number of voices in my head was deafening.

And then there was silence. I felt something move against my mind, brush against my soul as it inserted itself as a part of my consciousness. Big Red brushed up against me and pressed his very exposed body against mine as he put both of his hands against my face.

"I am Bastien Dante LeBlanc, Alpha of the Aces," he said as he moved one hand away from my face and gestured to the wolves around us. "And we want you to find our missing *frère*. Our brother. Our missing *soeur*. Our sister. And the *enfant de loup* she carries inside of her." He cast those yellow eyes down at me. "Or we will tear this city apart. *Sang pour le sang. D'accord, mon amie?*"

I didn't need my mom to translate for me, nor did I need the echo of their meaning in my head through the link the Alpha had just forced on me. They were desperate to find their pack mates, especially the wolf child their sister carried. And if they didn't find her alive, Mr. LeBlanc, the Alpha of an *actual* Werewolf pack, would declare war on the city of New Orleans.

Blood for blood.

* * *

Continued in Elemental Moon!

Thank you for purchasing and reading Elemental Shadows. It would be greatly appreciated if you could take a moment and leave an honest review of this book within the guidelines of your favorite retailer.

If you want to be notified when Phaedra's next novel is released and get free stories and occasional other goodies, please sign up for her mailing list by going her website at phaedraweldon dot com.

Your email address will never be shared and you can unsubscribe at any time.

Glossary

Pronunciations:
Crwys - *Cruise*
Medbh - *Mayv*
Sidhe - *Shee*
Dijin - *Gin*
Alfheim - *Alf-hime*

Definitions:

Magical Parliament - a grouping of thirteen High Witches chosen from all over the world to regulate magic use and the teaching of magic so as to avoid revealing a Witch's presence to the Cowen world. There are more than thirteen High Witches at any given time, but only thirteen are chosen to serve in Parliament.

Demon Realms - worlds that exist outside and yet beside the Material Plane. Other names used for these realms are the Mental, Astral, Abysmal, Ethereal, Peripheral and sometimes *Alfheim*.

Mother's Tracker - The Parliament once granted tracking rights to some Elder Witches, especially those with Elemental Gifts. The last Tracker to officially receive this right was Samantha's mother, Elizabeth Hawthorne. The right gave them the ability to see, hear, taste, and smell trails left behind by a named target. This is the magic Eliza used to track Dionysus and made it impossible for the Leviathan to escape Eliza's abilities.

Elemental Witch - A God Mother's child who possess all five of the Elemental Gifts; Earth, Air, Water, Fire and Spirit. The combination of the elements make the use of Spirit possible, though small instances can be achieved with little training. Elementals use their own energy to power their magic as they transmute the magic inherent in the Material Plane into power.

Dianic Witch - A God Mother's child who does not possess any of the Elemental Gifts. Dianics are given Gifts such as second sight, telekinesis, telepathy, aural visions, clairvoyance and psychometry.

Elder Witch - A title given to any Witch possessing three Gifts, one usually required to be Elemental, who serves on the local counsels under a High Witch.

Magical Sight/Other Sight - the ability to see magic. All Witches possess this ability, but not all Cowens do. Those that can are usually slightly touched with a Dianic Gift.

Circle - Cutting the Circle is the Witch's ability to cut a circle into the Earth, thus creating sacred space for ritual.

Drawing Down the Moon - The ability of a Witch to join with the God Mother through Her blood in their veins. The phrase is also used by Dianic Witches when referring to creating sacred space.

Athame - Usually a black handled knife. The Witch's ceremonial knife. Represents the Witch's will.

Warlock - Often thought to be the term given to male witches. It's not. This is a state of banishment, when a Witch's connection to their magic is removed.

Hierarchy:
Cowens - Non magical folk.

Dianic Witches - God Mother's children possessing only Dianic gifts, such as telekinesis and psychometry.

Hedge Witch - God Mother's children whose Gifts contain an inherent, working knowledge of all of the Gaia's plants. They possess a very latent touch of all the Elements but not enough to wield them. They generate their magic through these combinations of herbs.

Elemental Witches - God Mother's children who possess all five of the Elemental Gifts.

Elder Witch - God Mother's children who possess at least one Elemental Gift but have dedicated themselves to their craft and their follow Witches for the betterment of all of the God Mother's children.

High Witch - A position voted upon; a position of leadership, and not one to take lightly. In order to be a High Witch, a God Mother's child must have at least two of the Elemental Gifts and one Dianic.

Cyber Witch - Still fairly unknown.

Author

Phaedra Weldon is a writer and mother of one. Born in Pensacola, Florida, Phaedra was raised in the lush, green southern tropic of Georgia. She grew up on southern ghost stories told while eating marshmallows around campfires, or on the back of pick-up trucks in the middle of cornfields on chilly October nights. Phaedra currently lives in the South with her daughter.